A dozen riders approached the ranch in a loose bunch. They spread out as they hit the yard, coming to a halt in a rough semicircle around the house. Frank watched with a professional eyes as half of them swung down and moved to investigate the buildings, returning a minute later with their report. He felt no surprise as they began tearing apart a haystack and piling the hay against the walls of buildings. The still mounted men threw their ropes over anything they could pull down, corral posts, front gate, well housing, and dragged them over to the barn. They wer thorough about it. There was to be nothing left of the Chain Link. Finally the torches were lit and they moved like fireflies around the yard.

DAY OF THE
AMBUSHERS

Stephen E. Fugate

MANOR
BOOKS
INC.

A MANOR BOOK

Manor Books, Inc.
432 Park Avenue South
New York, New York 10016

ISBN: 0-532-23158-9

Chapter 1

It rained the day they buried Jim Pierce. It was a fine, steady drizzle, caught by the shifting wind and whipped in under slanted umbrellas and into upturned coat collars. There were many of these on cemetery hill. A good man had died, a well-liked man. A whole town had turned out to pay its respects.

To the six men toiling slowly up the hill with the heavy wooden casket, the rain was almost welcome, helping mask emotions they might have found hard to hide. These six had been Pierce's closest friends:

Harvey Kinder, Little Harv, one time jockey now horse raiser, Pierce's nearest neighbor for a dozen years; and Judge Holman, whose daughter Pierce was to have married, led the way, letting their small size help keep the casket level as they moved along the slippery path.

Behind them came Doc Prentis and Troy Beasley. Prentis had also courted Margaret Holman, losing out to Pierce without losing his friendship. Beasley, like Joe White behind him, had known Pierce since childhood; had ridden with him on a score of roundups before deciding to live in town, Troy as storekeeper, Joe as blacksmith.

The final member of the sextet was the gambler, John Lovejoy. He had not known Pierce as long as had the others; yet, since he was a man who did not make friends easily, his sense of loss was as great as theirs.

Oddly enough, had the thoughts of these men at that moment been pieced together, the result would have been a picture of Jim Pierce's last twenty-four hours. These six, along with one other who was not here, had been part of, or witness to, almost every waking minute of that last day. They could have included his thoughts and feelings, also, they had been that close to him.

Harvey Kinder's foot slipped on the soft mud. He swore softly as he caught his balance and steadied the heavy coffin. He swore at the reminder of the kind of man who had died; swore at the memories that crowded unasked into his thoughts. Was it only three days ago, Saturday, that he had reined in at the bridge and watched Jim ride down the trail from the pass?

In memory, at least, it seemed that the strength and vitality of the big man, the sheer love of living, had easily spanned the distance between them. Harvey had waited where he was as Jim dropped down from the ridge and, riding with his characteristic easy confidence, urged his reluctant mount down the steep bank to the road.

Together they crossed the bridge, their horse's

6

hoofs drumming loudly on the heavy planks. Below them, the rushing water growled around the trestle supports; dark water in a dark mood, pushing ill-temperedly at everything in its path. This was the back door to town and, like so many back doors, was drably ugly. The buildings facing River Street thrust out over the river bank, resting their bustle-like rears on heavy pilings. The bolder ones stood well out in the current, their feet circled with cuffs of white foam, or barnacled with bits of brush. Beneath them all was a heavy deposit of water-swept trash.

The two men paused a moment to watch a drifting log, pushed by the full force of the current, hurl up a geyser of fine spray as it crashed into a projecting rock. It hung there an instant, then swung slowly out and around until it tore free and started on again, gathering speed as it passed under them.

Kinder said, "She's sure a heller in the spring, ain't she? Hard to believe y'could wade 'cross come August. Makes me thirsty just watchin' it. How 'bout it?"

"Have to shave and change. I'm having dinner with Judge Holman."

"Ha! Y'mean Margaret Holman, don't ya'?"

Jim grinned. "I imagine she'll be there."

"Y'got time for a couple, three beers."

"Maybe a short one, Harv."

They turned into River Street and angled across it toward the Nugget. There was little activity on the street. A freight wagon lumbered slowly toward them, its driver half asleep on the seat, while across the way a pair of firemen worked dreamily on the brass fittings of their engine. The only horses in sight was a group of eight in front of the Staghorn saloon.

Kinder nodded at these. "Lot of the J.C. hands in town for this early."

"Not too surprising. Colter's put on quite a number of extra hands lately. Not working hands, though."

"I can see that."

They pushed into the cool dimness of the barroom,

empty except for the bartender. Pierce lifted two fingers, made a motion as though pulling a beer spigot and watched as the two beers slid down the bar.

Kinder said, "Y'figure the J.C. ranch hands are going to make trouble?"

Pierce spun the heavy mug between his palms, watching its contents climb the glass walls to lap threateningly at the rim. "Mark isn't carrying a dozen extra hands for fun. Not the kind across the street, anyway."

"Could be a bluff. Wouldn't take much to scare Oncina out, an' the Hazels ain't exactly long on backbone."

"It's possible. You're right about Oncina and the Hazel Brothers, but Dave Martinson is a horse of a different color. He won't back down, and it's his Lazy M that Colter really had his eye on."

"Y'did fling a hitch into his plans when y'sided with Dave, right 'nough. He didn't figure on that. Reckon he figured to scare Starbuck into keeping' y'out of it. It's no secret your partner wanted to stay strictly neutral."

"Then he figured wrong. Jay won't be scared into or out of anything. He's agreed to go along with me on this."

"But if y'wasn't in the picture, he'd be out?"

"Possibly."

"Then damn it, man, where's that leave ya'? Colter's no fool. He knows how Starbuck thinks. If he's really plannin' somethin', he only has to get rid of y' to knock your Diamond Seven out of the picture."

Jim's answering shrug annoyed Kinder. "It's no joke. With a damn good chance the J.C. is really after your scalp, y'go traipsin' around the country side alone, without even a rifle in your saddleboot. That's practically beggin' for a bullet."

"It's not that bad, Harv. Mark wouldn't shed any tears if something happened to me, but it's not likely that he's declared open season either. You can't keep something like that a secret. Not with the number of

8

men he has, anyway."

"His crew don't have to know. Just one man with a rifle sittin' in the brush when y'come driftin' by, an' y'won't know what hit y'till y'wake up with a shovel in your hand an' the smell of sulphur all 'round." Kinder had a tendency to slur his words as he grew excited, and the last sentence would have been unintelligible to anyone but a close friend. Catching Jim's smile and understanding it, he gulped down the rest of his beer, took a deep breath and, spacing his words carefully, "How come ya' didn't have a rifle with ya'?"

"Stock got smashed. I sent it in to Svenson to have it fixed. Didn't want to haul two of them back with me." Jim drained the last swallow from his glass and asked casually, "You see Joe White today?"

"No, I..." The change of subject was too abrupt. Kinder stopped and looked up suspiciously. "How'd it get broke?"

Once Harvey had smelled an evasion, he wouldn't be put off. Jim's smile became wry. "A bullet," he said. "Someone threw a shot at me."

Chapter 2

Judge Holman felt the shift of weight as Harvey's foot slipped and braced himself against it. He didn't need it to remind him of the man Jim Pierce. He had only to close his eyes to see him as he was the last time they had been together—was it only three days ago, Saturday—sitting opposite him at the dinner table. He could see it as clearly as though he was back there again.

The women folk had finished clearing the table, and the cigars were being passed around. Jim took one and sniffed it appreciatively as he passed the humidor on to the Judge's younger brother, Will, who showed the pipe he was taking from his pocket, by way of refusal. Jim passed the humidor on to the eldest brother Tom. It was in honor of one of his rare visits that Sunday's dinner had been moved forward.

Tom accepted with a nod of thanks and, completely straight faced, passed them on to the Judge's son, Glynn.

With attempted casualness, the boy said, "No

thanks, I'm still eat..." Then, seeing the twinkle in the others eye, he added," Aw, you know I don't smoke."

"Then how about another piece of cake instead?"

"Well..." the boy grinned his thanks as he looked hopefully at his father.

The Judge shrugged helplessley saying."All right, one more, but take it outside with you. We have some talking to do."

"Aw, can't I..."

"No. Outside with you, now" He watched as the boy cut another generous piece, it was his third, and wondered where the devil he put it. In height, he supposed. At thirteen, the boy was already taller than he, although as slender as a bean. In this respect, the boy resembled his older brother more than he did his father, a fact that left the Judge with mixed feelings. He was glad to see the promise of at least average height for his son; but with every reminder of his brother's slim waistline, he became uncomfortably aware of his own expanding one. Both he and Will, who ran the general store in town, had been exposed to entirely too much of Alice's good cooking.

The Judge ran his hand across his vest thoughtfully and, with a regretful sigh, undid another button. He received some solace from the fact that Will was still one button ahead of him. When Glynn had made his reluctant departure, the Judge said, "What's this about you being shot at, Jim?"

"Where did you hear about that?"

"I ran into Harv just after you left him. He seemed to think the J.C. might have set it up."

"Hardly likely. I told him that."

"He's hard to convince"

"You're right there," Jim agreed. Leaning forward, he began to draw aimless patterns on the tablecloth with his fork. He was a man who had to keep his hands busy as he talked. "There's been a little rustling going on lately. Nothing serious, just annoying. Last week I cut some fresh sign, not a couple of hours old, where somebody was easing a dozen head back into

11

the hills. I followed it and caught up just this side of White Pond. I was starting to circle them when somebody opened up on me from the rim. It was a damn long shot, but he bounced a bullet off my rifle stock, smashing it to kindling. I pulled back into the timber like I'd seen the devil himself. I guess they pulled out the other way just as fast. I never even got a glimpse of them."

"No idea who they were then?"

"No. It wasn't the J.C., I'm sure of that. It was a fluke that I ran across their trail at all. If it had rained, as it threatened, I couldn't have followed it. They were probably counting on rain and got fooled."

"I'm not surprised that rustling should pick up just now. The vultures always seem to gather when there's trouble brewing. What do you think the chances are of keeping it from breaking out?"

"Hard to say. Fairly good I think, as long as we stick together. The J.C. can't afford a long fight. It's going to be hard keeping the Chain Link in line, though. Not that they would be much help if things got rough. Even if you count the boy, and he may be the toughest of the lot, there are only three men there. Mark's been putting pressure on Oncina all spring. Now, he's made him an offer."

"Oh? I hadn't heard that."

"Fifteen hundred, lock, stock and barrel."

"Fifteen hundred! Why that's robbery," the Judge said angrily. "But then he wouldn't need the kind of crew he has if it weren't, would he? Do you think Juan will sell for that? The Chain Link is no prize, but it's worth three times that."

"Easily. But fifteen hundred may look a lot bigger when it's carrying a 'take it or get nothing' threat. Particularly when he might lose the place legally, if Mark makes his lawsuit hold up."

"That's true," the Judge said. Then, noticing the puzzled expression on his brother's face, he added, "You haven't heard about this part of it, have you, Tom? Of course not. It happened after you were here

12

last time. Quite an interesting legal problem." Looking at the others, he asked, "Do you mind?"

Without waiting for an answer, he started right in. "I'll make it brief. Just before the war, Ed and Sarah Barret moved out here from Virginia. He knew what the war would do to the South and wanted no part of it. He sold everything back there and reinvested in land out along Wildman and Bear Creeks, and some along the Black Horse. Of course he used some open range, but he made sure he owned the most important areas outright. The whole place became the Hen Track."

The Judge paused to light another cigar, rolling it carefully in the match flame until it was glowing satisfactorily, then continued, "He must have used half a dozen attorneys during those years. I did some work for him, so did Abe Young and old Jim Nash. Yet with all that, it never seemed to occur to him to have us handle the incidental job of drawing up his and Sarah's wills. It just seemed so simple, he did it himself.

"I'll grant that they were simple. Each left everything to the other as survivor. The only difference between the two was where one was not survived by the other. Ed specified a division of property among his nephews, Henry and Sam, and Sarah's nephew, Mark. But she left everything to Mark. Well, to make a long story short, Ed and Sarah were both killed when their carriage went off the bridge at Hertz Ravine.

"When the wills were probated, the property was divided according to Ed's will and nobody thought about it. Mark took over the Bear Creek range and used his initials, J.C. as his brand. Mark is his middle name, you know.

"Henry was an established businessman back in Kentucky and sold his share sight unseen. Sam came out here, but had barely seen his windfall when he lost half of it in a poker game here in town. He sold the rest and went back east. Mark was the big winner in that game and took over most of what Sam lost. Some people say this is when he got the idea of reestablishing the Hen Track. Personally, I don't think so. I think it came later, when Doc Prentis happened to mention that Ed Barret had probably been killed instantly, while Sarah may have lived through the night. You can imagine the direction Mark's thinking took when he heard that."

The Judge was addressing Tom whose puzzled frown lasted only a moment. "You mean that with Ed dead, Sarah, even though dying, had survived him, so he had inherited the whole place?"

"Exactly. I can almost read Mark's mind. First, the thought that if she had only lived a little longer he would have gotten everything; then the growing conviction that he should have anyway. For a few hours she had owned the Hen Track, and he was her heir; as simple as that."

"Would a claim like that hold up in court?"

"I won't say it's impossible, since I'm sure I could find a precedent if I had to, but I doubt if Mark is counting on it. In the first place, we're a little less influenced by precedent than your tradition-ridden eastern courts, especially since it's those same courts to which we would have to look for precedent. Second, proving order of death won't be easy."

"Oh? Isn't your Doctor Prentis a good man?"

The Judge said quickly, "There's not a better doctor between here and Saint Louis. Maybe none as good. He's quick, cool, particularly in an emergency, and knows what he's about every minute. Besides that, he's absolutely honest."

As Tom was considering this flat statement, the Judge reached across the table for the remainder of the cake and began to work a large walnut free of the icing. When it was loose, he popped it into his mouth with an air of triumph and carefully erased the evidence with the handle of a fork. "Now where was I? Oh, yes. As sure of himself as Dan is when he's doing something, he's just as unsure when it comes to

14

talking about it. A child can come down with measles in a family where there's already three cases. He'll treat it as measles, watch it run its course and see the child recover. Yet, never once will he say it was measles. It 'appears to be', or 'in my opinion anything else is unlikely', et cetera. He's like that with everything, including comments on the weather."

"The Judge is exaggerating a little," Jim said. "Even with Dan a broken leg is a broken leg and..."

"If it's a compound fracture with the bone projecting at least three inches," the Judge interjected wryly.

"...and a dead man is dead," Jim continued, ignoring the interruption.

"After the funeral, maybe," said the Judge, getting in the last word and receiving an amused gesture of surrender from Jim. "This has become a trademark with Dan, which I imagine he rather enjoys and it has become a habit."

"Yet supposing he could be pinned down to a definite answer. Could Colter possibly win?" Tom asked.

The Judge spread his hands palms up. "It's not impossible."

"Then wouldn't he wait before trying force?"

"He could think his chances are better if he has possession, as they might be; or even better if there is no one around to contest the claim. On the other hand, this could all be a bluff designed to encourage the weaker ones to sell out cheaply."

"You don't think it is?"

"Oh, he'd be happy enough to have it scare someone into quitting. The fact that he made Oncina an offer indicates that, but he knows Dave Martinson and a couple of the others won't quit without a fight. While Jim may have made him change some of his plans, I don't think he has made him give them up. No, I see it as just a part of the overall scheme. In the first place, as Jim says, it puts added pressure on the weaker ones. Secondly, it will serve as justification for whatever he does. Mark knows people; knows they'll usually go along with a winner. If he becomes the big man on this range, it won't be long before people will say that he only took what was rightfully his; that he would have won it in court if he could have gotten a fair deal. Pretty soon they'll start believing it themselves."

"You're being a little cynical, Judge," Will said.

"Maybe. But I know people, too. Oh, I don't say everyone will forget—just most of them. They'll distort events and justify actions, let time dim their resentment; personalities cloud the issues. The less justification there seems to be, the longer it will take, but it will happen. Mark won't want public feeling too strongly against him if he can help it, but he won't let it stop him." The Judge looked pointedly at Jim with the last words.

Jim shrugged. "You still have to do what you have to," he answered casually. A half an hour later, he went for a walk with Margaret. It was the last time the Judge saw him alive.

Sometime later, when dusk had fallen and full dark was only minutes away, John Lovejoy stepped out onto River Street and moved leisurely along toward the heart of town. It had grown cool now that the sun was down and the lamplight, falling gently from doorway and window, marked the earth with yellow squares which seemed to promise a warmth they did not posses.

Lovejoy held to the middle of the street until a group of riders moved up behind him, forcing him up onto the board walk. He watched idly as they searched the crowded rails for a place to tie their mounts and, finding none, swung into State Street and out of his sight. He moved to the corner and stood undecided on the walk, watching the steady flow of the Saturday night crowds.

Across the street the Palace's four piece orchestra laid a heavy accent on the three-four rhythm of a waltz which mixed, if not blended, with the throaty voice of the Gem's soprano soloist, engaged in a determined search for exact pitch. From an open window behind him, came the dry clatter of poker chips and the soft whir of shuffling cards. Accenting the steady drone of voices, came the chant of the roulette table's croupier, "The winner is eighteen, black. Eighteen, black."

Near the edge of town a gun roared, five even shots, and Lovejoy watched a deputy step from his post across the street and turn toward the sound, moving without haste. His pace indicated that he recognized the sound for what it was; a revolver emptied at the sky by some already drunken cowhand.

Finally, Lovejoy turned and bucked the stream of traffic to the entrance of the Palace bar. He pushed through the swinging doors and eyed the crowded bar. At the far end he saw Jim Pierce, hand making a circling gesture above his head. There was a drink waiting for him when he reached the place Jim had managed to make between himself and the wall. Pierce said, "How are you, John?"

"Same as last time, just a month older."

"Aren't we all, John?"

"Yes, but I've got twenty years lead on you." Only his grey hair did not belie his claim. His face was firm and unlined without hint of sallowness, his figure slender and erect.

"You're not dealing tonight?"

Lovejoy shook his head. "Not tonight. We're having a stud game upstairs at nine. Care to sit in?"

"No thanks. I have to be up early tomorrow. I think I'd rather see the sun rise after I get up than before I get to bed."

"Shouldn't be as bad as that, the game's called for two."

"That's what they said the last time. But by the time anyone noticed it was two, it was past three. Then there was the longest 'half hour more' I ever saw, plus four or five 'last rounds'. I got out in time for

17

breakfast. It will be the same tonight."

Lovejoy's lips curved in a broad smile. "I hope not, but I'm afraid you're right."

Their attention was diverted by a brief scuffle at the other end of the bar, which ended with the hurried, unwilling exit of an aggressive drunk. Lovejoy said, "You have any trouble with Ben Dutcher lately?"

"No, why?"

"He's in town, Jim, and geared for trouble. He's already made a few hardly complimentary remarks."

Pierce shrugged easily. He's done that before."

"Not like this. He'll be hard to ignore if you should happen to run into him."

"Probably just liquor talk," Jim said. "I ran into him with Mark as they were coming in. He could have said something then." This wasn't quite true. Whatever his faults, Dutcher would not have started trouble in front of a woman and Margaret had been with Jim when they met. They had been strolling along the river road when they met Colter and his foreman, Ben Dutcher, on their way into town. The two men reined in and Dutcher reached up to touch his hat brim as he inclined his head in Margaret's direction, before swinging around to stare at Jim. Colter went further. Sweeping his hat off, he said, "Good afternoon, Miss Holman; Jim."

Jim nodded and Margaret said cooly, "Good afternoon, Mr. Colter." She answered his questions about the rest of her family with cool politeness. A moment later they rode on.

There had been nothing more to it; except Dutcher's expression; antagonism, speculation and, possibly, anticipation. Antagonism, he expected. The J.C. foreman had never liked him. When he had taken a stand against the outfit to which Dutcher gave complete loyalty, dislike had become hatred. Nor was the speculating, weighing glance surprising. A brutally tough fighter, Ben wondered how he would make out against someone with an equal reputation. It was the suggestion of anticipation that distrubed Jim. It had been only a flash of expression and Jim convinced himself that he had imagined it. Now, he wondered.

Lovejoy pulled his watch from his vest pocket and snapped open the cover. His eyebrows lifted slighlty. "Getting late. Time I was getting up there."

They pushed through the crowd to the door where Jim said. "Luck, John," casually.

Just as casually, Lovejoy said, "Take care." It was the last thing he ever said to Jim Pierce.

Troy Beasley was locking the door of his store when he saw Pierce leave Lovejoy and come toward him. He waited there until the other reached him and shook hands warmly. "Ah'm goin' t' have one beer afore ah hit the sack. How 'bout it?" His accent, soft and slightly nasal, spoke strongly of a Tennessee he had left nearly twenty years before.

"Guess one more won't hurt me. Let's make it Bauer's, though. The Palace is crowded as hell."

They moved along the walk, Jim leading the way. He reached the swinging doors and pushed one inward, turning as he did to speak to Beasley. Here, fate took over. On the other side, Ben Dutcher was striding toward the doorway, his head turned as he threw a parting remark over his shoulder. His left arm stretched out for a door which suddenly swung inward under his groping hand to catch him solidly in the armpit, stopping him in midstride. As he rebounded from the door edge, he twisted around in a violent effort to retain his balance, but his legs tangled with a chair and he fell heavily, bringing a nearby poker table down with him.

Pierce made an effort to head off trouble. "Sorry, Ben," he said, and extended his hand to help the other up.

19

Dutcher was not one to take exception to every jostling. He almost took the proffered hand before recognizing its owner. He struck Jim's hand aside. "You son of a bitch! You dirty..." He stopped there, as though recognition had just come. "Oh, it's Jim Pierce," he continued, his voice rich with sarcasm. "Big man Pierce. Still throwing your weight around."

"An accident, Ben," Jim said mildly.

"Accident hell!" Dutcher flung the table violently aside and climbed to his feet slowly. "It's just like I been saying. You don't look where you're going because everybody's supposed to get out of your way. You're so God damned big and important, we're supposed to jump when you say the word. Well, not me, brother. I'm just going to see how big you really are."

The preamble out of the way, he started forward; big, tough, dangerous. The barman's pleading, "Please, Ben," went unnoticed.

Further talk was useless. Dutcher wanted this fight and, for some reason, was determined to have it now. Pierce shook his head and said flatly, "Not here, Ben. I'll be over to Shultz's corral in five minutes." He turned his back and rested his elbows on the bar.

The oval bar mirror was a small one and he could see only one arm and shoulder of the J.C. foreman in it. He kept his eyes on this, tense and ready. There was a long silence, then Dutcher said, "All right, bastard, five minutes." He stamped out. A minute later, there was a concerted rush for the door.

Chapter 3

Even at night, Shultz's corral made an excellent arena. It lay between the R.B. Hays House, whose big windows threw their light across the intervening drive to illuminate half the corral, and the Palace Hotel. The latter's side windows were less bright, but someone had hung a row of lanterns along the fence. The big, brass lamps at each side of the stable entrance were glowing brightly.

If Joe White, telling Lovejoy about it next morning at breakfast, was guilty of describing feelings, both mental and physical, as though he were a participant, the fact was graciously overlooked by the gambler. White was a frail man who, by his own admission, couldn't fight his way out of the proverbial paper bag. But he became so emotionally involved in any fight he witnessed, it was a standing joke that he was more bruised than either fighter. Knowing both White and Pierce, Lovejoy was able to translate White's excited narration into a reasonably accurate picture of the action.

Dutcher was at the far end of the corral when Pierce stepped through the gate. They moved toward each other as though by signal; two big men, each with a reputation for toughness, well matched physically. If Dutcher had a slight edge in weight, Jim's six-foot three topped him by an inch.

Ben started it the second they were close enough. As though trying to end it with one blow, he swung a hard right at Jim's head, then checked it short and hooked a left to the body instead. He followed with right, but Pierce rolled away from its full power, at the same time crossing his own right to the head.

They circled a moment, sparring cautiously, but neither was inclined to waste time. Ben charged in and Pierce stepped forward to meet him, connecting with a solid blow to the body. He missed with another and took a hard smash in the chest that staggered him. Ben closed in then, trying to use the crushing power of his arms and shoulders. He got one arm around Jim's waist, but Jim caught the other before he could lock them together. For a dozen seconds the soft scrape of shoes on the hard-packed earth and their heavy breathing were the only sounds.

Abruptly, Ben leaned into Jim, dropping his arm to the back of Jim's knees in an attempt to lift him off his feet. Pierce was ready for it and brought his knee up hard into Ben's face, breaking them apart, hurling Ben back against the rail fence. It was the first break in the fight. Pierce leaped forward to take advantage of it. He underestimated Ben's speed. The foreman

22

bounced off the fence, came in like a battering ram under Jim's swinging right, and caught him shoulder first in the stomach to somersault him into the dust ten feet away.

Desperately he rolled over and scrambled to one knee, but the bull-like charge had thrown Dutcher to the ground, too. He was just getting to his feet.

Pierce rose slowly. A steel band seemed to be clamped around his chest, shutting off the air his lungs screamed for; making him helpless—and Dutcher was coming in. He backed away in a wide half circle until, finally, the band loosened and his breath came back with a shuddering sigh.

They came together violently to stand toe to toe, slugging with raw savagery, each taking what came in an effort to beat the other down with brute force. Neither was successfully, and Pierce changed tactics abruptly. Tackling Ben low, he half lifted him from his feet and drove him, with board splintering force, into the stable wall. As they broke apart, he swung his elbow in a short, wicked arc to the side of Ben's neck and followed with a hammerlike backhand blow on the head.

He blocked an up-driving knee only by taking its full force on the muscles of his thigh. An agonizing pain shot through the full length of his leg, and when he put his weight on it, it buckled slightly, throwing him off balance. In that second something like a granite block came out of the darkness and caught him on the temple, spinning him completely around.

Somehow he was on the ground, rolling desperately along it. He seemed to be enveloped in a gray mist, pinpointed with dancing lights and there was a roaring sound in his ears. He got as far as his hands and knees when, from the mists, a hazy shape moved toward him. Instinct made him throw himself at it, bringing Ben down on top of him. He locked his arms around Ben's legs and hung on grimly, taking a merciless rain of blows about the back and shoulders as he waited for the mist to clear.

23

The ringing was still in his ears when they finally got to their feet, but the haziness had left and his eyes would focus. Still, he took a couple of hesitant backward steps. Ben misunderstood and rushed in. Ready for it, Pierce ducked under the looping right and stopped him short with a vicious left to the body. Ben's guard came down and, for an instant, his jaw was an open target for the tremendous blow Jim swung at it. It was as hard as he had ever hit a man and it sent Dutcher crashing back into the stable wall again. Pierce didn't follow up immediately, but stood rubbing the knuckles of his numbed hand, waiting for Dutcher to crumple to the dust.

He felt a distinct shock when, instead of falling, Ben braced himself against the wall and struggled erect, shaking off the effects of the blow. Swearing softly to himself for missing his chance, Pierce started forward, then stopped short. Dutcher's groping hand had found something leaning against the stable wall, and without conscious thought he had brought it up in front of him; a deadly, four tined hayfork, He stared at it, first uncomprehendingly, then with a gradual realization of the vicious weapon he had.

But Ben Dutcher was a proud man. Without pride he was nothing. There were no rules here, no one to stop him, but he had made his boast; what he would do, and how. If there had been no one within a thousand miles he would have had to do it that way. He threw the fork aside angrily and, with a strength drawn from his anger, hurled himself at Jim, driving him back step by step for the full length of the corral. Here, Pierce managed to hold his ground and they stood there slugging each other in an orgy of punishment that could not last.

Finally Dutcher's borrowed energy ran out. His punches lost their snap and he began to miss as often as he hit. In the end, he missed with a wild swing that threw him completely off balance. He was wide open. Jim gathered his own fading strength and brought another crashing blow to the jaw. Ben fell back

24

heavily against the fence yet, again, he refused to go down, and again Jim did not follow up. This time because he could not find the strength.

They stood like that, a dozen feet apart, Pierce swaying on rubbery legs; Dutcher holding himself up by one arm hooked over the top rail of the fence. At last, Jim took an uncertain, shuffling step forward.

Ben straightened slowly, his chest heaving, and his mouth slack. He said, "All right. All right." Turning, he pushed opened the corral gate, stepped through and moved along the fence to the hotel porch, his body carefully erect. He climbed the three steps to the porch and passed from sight across the face of the hotel. Only then did his step falter. He stumbled and fell against the wall of the next building, then dropped to his knees on the plank walk. Slowly he pulled himself to his feet and plodded on with weary, shambling steps.

Lovejoy had time to order breakfast, polish off a plate of bacon and eggs and start on his second cup of coffee before White ran out of breath. At that, Beasley could only wedge in a brief, "It were a wicked one, all right, real wicked," before White went on, "I can't figure Dutcher, though. Never thought he'd quit as long as he could stand. Not that I liked him much, but I never thought he was short on guts."

"Then I wouldn't change that opinion if I were you," Lovejoy said. He selected another biscuit from a napkin covered plate and began to butter it. "He didn't quit as long as he could lift a hand and, if he took the kind of beating you say, he wouldn't have been afraid of one more punch."

"Then why didn't he take it?" Joe asked, "'stead of lettin' everybody think he'd lost his guts."

"I doubt if he worries about what people think. And personally I think it took more courage to do it his way—and certainly more sense."

"Maybe you're right," White admitted grudgingly. "He sure didn't have much left, I guess. Floyd Bauer seen him tryin' to get on his horse after. Said as how

25

he couldn't make it. Had to climb up on to the trough first."

"It were a wicked one, all right," Beasley repeated. "Jim couldn't make it to Joe's place under his own steam."

A train whistle moaned for the crossing a half mile from town. Mechanically Lovejoy pulled the heavy gold watch from his vest and snapped it open. "Only ten minutes late."

"I don't like it," White growled. "When they start runnin' trains on time, a place is gettin' too damn civilized." Through the window, he caught sight of the short, fleshy figure of Everett Carpenter hurrying toward the restaurant. He nodded at it. "When Everett moves like that, somethin's up."

A second later Carpenter entered the room and came directly to their table. Without preamble, he said, "Any of you know Frank Adams if'n you seen him?" He didn't look at them, but kept his gaze on the street outside.

"I sat in a game with him in Hays City a couple of years ago," Lovejoy said. Reading the other's intent look, he added, "Why? Is he in town?"

"Ain't sure, only seen him once and... there, on the roan, take a look." He pointed at a rider just turning the corner into River Street; a moderately tall, slender man, strongly built in a lithe, graceful way, but with nothing in either build or dress to draw more than casual attention. In a brown sack coat, smudged a little with train soot, and a white linen shirt; tight fitting brown pants, tucked into low heeled, spurless boots and neat gray stetson, he might have been a visiting sheriff or wandering gambler, a cattleman or horse trader, as readily as what he was: one of the deadliest gun fighters in the country.

The four men at the window watched in silence as he approached. He passed within a few feet of them, giving them a close look at his face. It was a dark face with deepset eyes and a straight nose above a thin, black mustache and a wide mouth, compressed

26

slightly as though afraid of smiling. It was neither handsome nor homely and not particularly memorable. Possible Lovejoy was the only man in town who could have positively identified him. "That's Adams, all right," he said. He settled back in his chair, considerably disturbed. "He came in on the train?" he asked at length.

Carpenter nodded. "Hired that roan from me. Said he'd be back with it this afternoon."

"Say where he was headed?"

"Asked for the road to Hortonville, that's all."

"Hell, if that's where he's headed there's nothin' to worry about," White said.

"Maybe. But a stranger heading for the J.C. would probably ask for the Hortonville road," Lovejoy said.

"Nothing much we can do." Lovejoy answered. "Other than finding out more definitely where he's headed for. Joe, can you circle around and reach the cutoff to the J.C. ahead of him?"

"Hell, if he's straddlin' one of those nags of Everett's, I could walk and still have to wait half an hour." He wasted no time getting started, however, pausing only long enough to nod in answer to Lovejoy's, "I'll either be here or at the Palace when you get back."

White returned shortly after lunch, picked up Carpenter at the livery and located Lovejoy at the Palace, playing cribbage with Beasley.

"It was the J.C.?" the gambler asked. It was more a statement than a question.

"Straight as a die," White answered. He sat down, leaned his elbows on the table and looked from one serious face to the other. "What does it mean? Why would Mark bring in somebody like that with all the gunhands he's already got?"

"Pierce," Lovejoy said grimly. "Mark has to get him out of the way, or take on more than he can handle. None of those third raters of his could stand up to Jim. He'd eat them with their spurs on."

"Why would they have to face him? A bullet in the
27

back is surer and cheaper. Men like Adams come high."

"Mark's a careful man, Joe. Killing Jim would create a tremendous amount of ill will even if the killer got away. But supposing he were caught? There isn't a man on the J.C., except Dutcher, who wouldn't implicate Mark to save his own skin, and Mark knows it. The sheriff would serve the warrant, too, cousins or not. Murder is a lot harder to swallow than a gunfight."

"But everybody'll know Colter sent for Adams," Everett objected. "Wouldn't it be just the same?"

Lovejoy shook his head. "There's no proof of any connection. Of course we can tie Adams to the J.C. now, but they couldn't have anticipated that. It was a hundred to one shot that he could ride through here on a Sunday morning and be recognized, though I'm surprised Mark took even that much of a chance."

"I imagine he hopes to make it look like a personal quarrel between Jim and Adams. It could easily be true.

"He's an ambitious man. Perhaps driven by ambition. Jim is standing in his way."

"There ain't no chance we're wrong?" Beasley asked hopefully. "Ah mean...well...maybe we're jist borrowin' trouble. Maybe he's come fer somethin' else entirely."

White snorted scornfully, but Lovejoy answered seriously, "I hope so, but I hardly think so. It's the only thing that explains last night; Dutcher wanting to try his luck against Jim all of a sudden. It was too crude, as though he knew he was short of time."

It was a new thought to the others. They mulled it over in silence for a minute. Finally Carpenter sighed. "Figures I reckon," he said. "Question is, what can we do?"

Lovejoy spread his hands helplessly. "Warn Jim, of course, but it won't change things. Jim is not the kind to run from trouble. Otherwise..." he let the sentence hang.

"What about the Marshal?" White suggested.

"Nothing he can do until after there's trouble. We better tell him anyway. In fact it might be a good idea to let the whole town know. If Mark wants to keep it a secret, that might throw a small hitch in his plans." Looking at the grave and worried faces, Lovejoy added, "Let's not do any mourning yet. We could be all wrong and, even if we aren't, Jim's pretty good at taking care of himself."

Chapter 4

It wasn't only because he was inside that the seventh man was unconscious of the rain. Like the other six, his mind was on the events culminating in the death of Jim Pierce.

He sat on the edge of the bed in his hotel room, staring at the rain streaked window, but seeing instead that Sunday afternoon, two days ago—only two days, it seemed longer—when he had ridden back to town from the J.C.. The first thing he noticed was the change in the town's attitude. When he had ridden through in the morning there had been only the normal curiosity about a stranger. Now there was an unmistakable hostility. Groups along the side walk fell silent as he drew near, while others turned to follow him with their eyes.

He returned his rented horse to a hostler who could not quite hide his dislike and, minutes later, ordered a beer from a bartender who didn't really try to. Turning, he hooked his elbows over the edge of the bar and watched the half curious, half antagonistic stares fall away. Someone had been busy. Everyone in town knew he was here. He finished his drink and moved to the street, leaving behind a rising murmur of voices. At the Palace Hotel's porch, he paused to light a cigarette and, at the same time, survey the street.

Directly across from him, a trio of women eagerly discussed the latest styles in a milliner's window, while above them, only a few yards away, yet in an entirely different world, several of the Nugget's girls caught the last warmth of the afternoon sun on the saloon's rear balcony. Further down the street, a trio of youngsters burst from the mouth of an alley, raced down the street, and disappeared around the far corner.

A group of armchair politicians interrupted their talk as they saw him and were staring coldly at him when another man stepped from the hotel, crossed the porch and descended the front steps. The watchers flicked their gaze to him then, almost in unison, swung it back to Adams, marked now with a sudden, sharp tension. He didn't need Colter's description to identify Jim Pierce. They might as well have called his name.

Their glances met in a brief, impersonal inspection, then Pierce stepped into the street and crossed to the far walk. The tension began to ease. Taking a final drag on his cigarette, Adams flipped it out into the road and turned into the hotel. It was early for dinner, but the dining room was open and, having nothing better to do, he took a table by the front window, ordered and ate his supper.

Leaving the dining room, he walked slowly out State Street until he came to the double tracks of the railroad. There was nothing on the other side but the picket fences and flowered yards around the half dozen frame houses lining the street and beyond this, the white spire of a church shining brightly in the last rays of the setting sun. The nearly deserted street was still light, but the deeper doorways and under-stair areas were becoming crowded with a dusty dark.

He turned back, walking slowly, and in the middle of the block paused to roll another cigarette. He lit up and leaned back against the end of a hitching rack as he smoked. An ancient Conestoga, so weathered that only the faintest trace of blue remained to prove its original color, rolled clumsily down the street, to come to a stop in front of the general store across from him. He watched the driver pull in close to the walk, climb stiffly from the seat, and begin to unhitch his team.

Since the store was closed, he considered this with a casual curiosity, deciding finally that it was being left there over night to be either loaded or unloaded in the morning. The high canvas top kept him from guessing which. The teamster finished unhitching and led his animals around the wagon and into the alley between the store and a narrow, one story building which, according to the black and gold sign beside its door, housed the office of Danial L. Prentis, M.D..

The alley ran completely through the block, and the dull thudding of the team's hoofs rang hollow for the full distance, ending abruptly as the team turned into Pine Street. It was then that Adams saw Jim Pierce again. The rancher rounded the nearby corner and angled across the street toward the freight wagon and the doctor's office beyond on a line which would bring him within a few feet of Adams.

He sensed that Pierce recognized him immediately for there was no sign from the man himself either in expression or step. He felt an instant admiration for this man, whom the town was so sure he had come to kill. He wondered what they would think if they knew he had refused the job. Probably believe he was afraid.

It was hardly that, it was a tendency to make snap judgements; to take an instant like or dislike for a person or thing, as he had just now with Pierce. In exactly the same way, he had liked neither Colter nor his proposition. Spontaneously, he made a completely

32

uncharacteristic gesture. He moved his hand a few inches from his gun. A trifling gesture, it was unmistakably a peaceful one. Pierce rounded the rear of the wagon and drew near the alley. The shot came then. Two closely spaced shots, striking out from the shadow at the alley mouth. Adams saw Pierce tremble as the bullets struck. Saw him stagger and fall to his knees. Saw him try vainly to lift his gun and, failing, pitch forward into the dust.

He had drawn his own gun with the sound of the shots. There was no target. He made a quick estimate and drove two bullets into the thin clapboard walls of the building. The ring of bullet striking metal doomed his hope that there would be nothing between the walls to turn the shots. He ran forward until he was opposite the alley. Halfway along the passage a shadowy figure was just twisting into the cross alley behind the doctor's office. He fired another snap shot, saw the man stagger slightly and knew he had scored some kind of hit.

He didn't follow, an alley like that could be a death trap for anyone not familiar with it. He turned to the fallen man. Dropping to one knee, he lifted a limp wrist and felt for a pulse. There was none. Jim Pierce was dead.

As he stood up, the town began to close in around him in a gradually thickening circle; the shocked and the angry, the excited and the dismayed and, as ever, the morbidly curious. One man bent down, turned the body over and felt for a heart beat. He looked up at the marshal, who had just pushed to the center of the circle, and shook his head.

A sigh went through the crowd. The marshal's chilly ice blue eyes lifted to meet Adams'. He answered their cold challenge with a nod toward the alley. "From there," he said. "Two shots. The last three were mine. Two into the wall, one at someone by the back corner. The last one may have hit." He said nothing more, but began ejecting the shells from his Colt, the unfired as well as the empties, holding them out for the marshal and the neck-craning townsmen to see.

Near the alley mouth someone called importantly, "There's a couple o' bullet holes here, right 'nough." The neck-craners turned that way.

On the other side, the circle gave way before the sudden pressure of someone forcing her way violently through. Not until she had almost reached the center, was Margaret Holman recognized and a belated effort made to stop her. She pushed by the restraining arms until she was within the circle.

Her twice repeated cry of, "Jim, Jim," was neither a scream nor a cry; hardly more than a whisper, yet filled with anguish and dispair. It froze the crowd, holding them motionless as she threw herself down beside Pierce's body. She pulled his head up into her lap, cradling it in her arms for a moment. Finally she looked up at the somber, uncomfortable circle around her, her eyes begging a help they could not give her. Then she saw Adams. All her emotions condensed into the single word of hate. "Murderer!" she screamed. "Murderer! Murderer!"

Pierce's unused pistol lay in the dust beside her hand. Her trembling fingers touched it, recognized it, and her hatred burst into the flame of violence. She swung it up, fingers already on the trigger, thumbs fighting back the hammer. Behind him, a section of the circle fell away like pins on a bowling alley and, in an instant, he stood alone. He was too close to pray that she would miss; a step too far away to do other than pray. He could only watch, almost dispassionately, as the hands holding the gun brought it up to chest level, the fingers tightened on the trigger; the hammer rock back and slip from under the thumbs. He could even think, quite objectively, that he wouldn't be in time as the marshal's hand drove down at the leveled forty-five. Nor would he have been, except that the fleshy edge of his hand hit in front of the falling hammer, checking it an eighth of an inch short of death.

Slowly Adams began to breathe again. His nerves

34

came to a trembling life which he fought to control while the marshal freed his hand from the pinch of the gun hammer and dabbed at a trickle of blood with his handkerchief. Someone else began to push into the crowd, one hand buttoning a neat black coat across a heavy chest, the other pushing a worn leather bag before him, as though it was a key to the circle's center.

"Too late for you, Doc," someone murmured.

The Doctor knelt beside the body, put his hand on it for a moment, then got slowly to his feet, his face pale and angry. He turned to the girl, still staring fixedly at Adams with a mixture of shock and hate. Gently he turned her face toward him, breaking her intent, almost hypnotized stare.

"He didn't do it, Margaret," he said. He had to repeat it twice before he could make her shocked mind understand. The tears came then in a sudden rush. He drew her close, protectively, as he answered the marshal's questioning look.

"I saw it from my office. I'd just returned from seeing Joe Fisher's wife and was hanging up my coat by the window. I looked out and saw him," he inclined his head slightly in Adam's direction, standing over by the rail. Just then Jim came around the corner. The first shots came from the alley."

"You're sure?

"Absolutely. The last ones were his, but he hadn't touched his gun before the shots from the alley, I'm sure of that. I heard someone run down the alley and across the back of my place. I tried to see who it was, but by the time I got the back door open, I'd lost any chance to catch him."

"You didn't see him at all?"

"Sorry Mac, not even a glimpse."

The marshal shrugged. "Maybe it was best, Doc. He might of seen you, too. One killing's enough."

Chapter 5

Those who observed Frank Adams at breakfast the following morning were, convinced that he was completely unconcerned with what the town might think of him, or whether they even accepted the fact that he had had nothing to do with Pierce's death. They were wrong. Behind his mask of indifference, he was very conscious of the town's opinion. He had been used, that much was certain, whether by plan or spontaneously he didn't know, and there had probably been the hope of using him as a scapegoat.

But for a reliable eyewitness, he might have been blamed. Even now he was going to be associated with the crime to some degree. Regardless of the Doctor's statement, some people would still suspect him or, more likely, say that he had been afraid of Pierce and used an accomplice.

He tried to convince himself that it didn't matter. He would be leaving town in a few hours and could leave it all behind. Yet he knew it would follow him. He had his own pride. The idea of being associated with this kind of killing galled him. He could not seem to force it from his mind.

As he left the dining room and stepped to the walk, he was more sensitive than usual about the town's attitude; the increased hostility and suspicion of the glances. Anger at the unknown ambusher increased the more he thought about it.

He walked out State Street to the railroad, then left along Union. There were buildings on only one side, the railroad on the other, beyond a narrow, raised strip of grass which someone had made an effort to beautify with two circular beds of flowers, their bright colors dimmed by a veil of soot.

The station was beyond the last building across the tracks. Adams walked down to it, crossed the high, gravel road bed, and stepped up to the platform. He hesitated an instant to stare southward along the rails, trying to find something attractive in those lonely places he would be returning to when he left Benton's Ford. He found none.

The station was a single room affair, divided into two unequal parts by a counter at the left of the door. On the right, a well polished, wooden bench ran along the three walls of the waiting room, ending beside the opposite door. In a sand filled square in the center of the floor, stood a squat, pot bellied stove; a cold and graceless monster just now. A small bulletin board, with its handful of faded notices, was the only other furnishing at this end of the room.

The steady clatter of a telegraph sounder came

from the other side of the counter. Adams turned that way and came upon the human counterpart of the stove behind him. The man was so enormously fat that everything in the room was dwarfed by comparison. The reinforced stool on which he sat was oversized, but still his tremendous buttocks flared out on all sides, completely obscuring the top.

Without looking up, he raised a surprisingly delicate hand to acknowledge Frank's presence, while continuing to receive the incoming message. Idly Adams tried to read it, but found it just too fast. A minute later the clicking stopped. The fat man shifted his hand to his own key to send an answer with an even faster touch.

Only then did he look up. "Howdy," he said. He heaved himself up from the stool and came over to the counter.

"When's the next train south?" Adams asked.

"One thirty, when it's on time."

"Usually on time?"

"Nope. Usually 'bout an hour late."

He waddled down the counter to where a partition, complete with grilled window, rose an additional four feet to form, according to the gilt lettering above the window, the "Passenger Ticket Office." "Where to?" he asked.

His smug assurance irked Adams. The whole attitude seemed to say, "Just as we figured, earned your blood money and now you're running."

He felt a sudden urge to be perverse. "I'll let you know when I decide to leave," he said shortly.

The fat man's eyebrows lifted in surprise. "Sure, sure," he said quickly. "I'm al'ays here when a train's due."

Moving aimlessly now, Adams turned down Pine Street on the third leg of his circuit of the block. It was much the same as Union, on one side a few stores, the post office and the jail, opposite them, nothing but corrals and waggon yards.

Halfway down the block, he came to an alleyway

38

and realized that it must be the other end of the one from which Pierce had been shot. On impulse he turned into it. A newspaper office, marked by the steady whoosh-thud of its flat-bed press, flanked it on one side. On the other was a closed silent warehouse; a deep building, almost touching the rear of the general store behind it.

The alley made a right angle turn for a few feet, then turned again to run out to State Street. None of the other buildings were as deep as the warehouse, so there was a winding, uneven passage behind them for the rest of the block. The killer had turned this way. Frank could picture him scurrying along it in the gathering dark, pausing in some especially dark shadow, gun in hand, in case he was followed. Even in daylight, Frank could see a dozen good places. He was glad he hadn't followed.

Behind one of the stores, a bad bit of drainage had left a soft, muddy strip across the path. Someone had bridged it with an old door. It made a loud squelch as his weight hit it and a softer sucking as it sprang back. A nearly full rain barrel stood a few inches from a nearby building corner, a perfect spot for a killer to wait. A careful examination of the ground around it showed nothing that might not have been made as easily by a dog drinking from the barrel as by a man kneeling there. He had hoped to find some trace of blood on the path, he was sure he had hit the killer with his last shot. A shallow wound, apparently, for the marshal had found nothing.

At the last building, a brick walk crossed the alley, giving exit to all three streets. Adams paused here, considering the murderer's probable actions. Finally he decided that, having been forced in one direction so long, he would want to turn here. Not to the left, where he would surely be seen by people running down State Street.

Frank turned right, back to Pine Street, but here he was stopped. Even if he had been right so far, there were a dozen new ways open and no choice among them. He hesitated a minute then, with a helpless shrug, gave up and circle back to the hotel.

The Palace Hotel was the only true three story building in town. Sitting on the sill of his third floor window, Adams was able to look across the roofs of the town and see the silver threads of the railroad tracks swing away from town to head straight north into the distant mountains. It was well after one thirty. He had eaten dinner and paid his hotel bill. Behind him, on the bed, his bag was packed and ready.

He sat in the warmth of the sun and watched a cloud of smoke gradually draw near. Then the train itself crawled into sight. He sat in the window and listened to the low moan of its whistle at the distant crossing and, minutes later, the slowing chug of the engine and shrill squeal of wheel flanges biting into the rail at the curve just beyond town. The train slid into the station, coming to a stop with a metallic clank of couplings and the sharp and was gone. Adams still sat there in the window.

By not taking the train, he had made a decision, although not certain exactly what. He knew only that he would stay here until he could prove one thing to the town; that he had had nothing to do with the killing of Jim Pierce.

Sitting in the same drab hotel room the following morning, and somehow more conscious of its loneliness than ever, Adams was little closer to any definite course of action. In the afternoon, when the rain had eased to an intermittent drizzle, he crossed to the courthouse where a surprised young clerk pointed out the various land holdings in the valley on a big, hand drawn map. His own curiosity made him a veritable fountainhead of information. By the time Frank left, he had a clear picture of the north end of the valley; the people who ranched there, the places they ran, the men who rode for them. A vague idea began to form.

Next morning he bought a horse and rode north toward Juan Oncina's tiny Chain Link. Halfway there, he heard riders on the trail ahead and pulled off into the brush to watch Mark Colter ride by with three of his hands. Plainly they had been to see Oncina. With Pierce dead, Mark was wasting no time.

The Chain Link was a little different from a thousand other small ranches. A sturdily built three room house, somewhat weather beaten, a freshly painted barn, a small corral, two sheds and a covered well. Their varying state of repair reflected the usual tendency to maintain the working units before the living quarters.

The two figures on the porch, a stocky man of about forty and a boy in his early teens, fell silent as he pulled up at the steps and waited for the customary invitation to dismount. It was slow in coming. He didn't push it.

The man would be Juan Oncina, he decided, although there was little trace of the Spanish ancestry suggested by the name. His square, reddish face had more of a German or Scandinavian cast, and the boy, with his light hair and fair skin, appeared most decidedly Nordic. In both faces there was anger and resentment close to the surface and, in the older man at least, a bitter weariness. It was at him that Adams directed his steady gaze. The man met his look for several seconds, then his resistance died, and he murmured without cordiality, "Light. Light an' git in out'a the sun."

Dismounting, Frank looped the reins over the rail and climbed the four steps to the veranda. "My name's Adams. Frank Adams," he said simply.

The older man nodded. "Juan Oncina. My son Richard." No hand was offered.

There was a long, uncomfortable silence. Adams appeared not to notice as he pulled a tobacco sack from his pocket, extending it first to the man, who said, "No thanks," gruffly, then to the boy, who mumbled something then looked down at his shoes. Adams leaned back against the porch rail and carefully made his cigarette. The silence dragged on.

41

Finally, more to say something than to be hospitable, Oncina cleared his throat and said, "Ah...there's a little coffee on the stove...left from breakfast...still hot I reckon." When Frank accepted, he sent the boy in for it, admonishing him to, "Make sure it's hot." The boy entered the house. There was a low murmur of conversation, then a woman came and stood just inside the doorway. The rancher cleared his throat again. "You come to see me about somethin', Mr. Adams?"

Frank became interested in the smoke drifting up from his cigarette. "Saw Colter back on the road. He was here?"

The anger returned to Oncina's face; the bitterness to his voice. "He was here," he said vehemently. "Yeah, he was here, all right. Come to run me off my place, that's what! Said I'd better take his offer or I'd git run off an' won't git nothin'. Give me till Saturday to..." he stopped abruptly, anger draining away, as he realized he might be talking to the man who would have the job of running him off.

"What was the offer?"

Oncina was angry again. "Fifteen hundred. Fifteen hundred stinkin' dollars for all this!" He made a sweeping motion with his arm, a gesture Caesar might have made in referring to all Rome. For a moment, pride of ownership wiped out the look of defeat. Then the weariness returned.

Adams knew the answer to his next question before he asked. "Are you going to sell?"

The other lifted his hands in a vague, helpless gesture. "What else kin I do? I cain't fight him, he's got upwards of twenty-five men, there's only four of us, even countin' the boy, an' with Pierce gone..." Again he made the vague gesture, showing how much he had leaned on Pierce. The woman stepped through the door and put her hands on his shoulders, giving what comfort she could.

The boy returned with the coffee, followed by an older man, apparently the woman's father. Adams
42

asked, "There's no chance of help from the other places?"

"No." It was a positive statement by a man who would have clung to any hope. "With Pierce gone the Diamond Seven is out, Starbuck ain't the kind to worry much about other folk, and Martinson's only got seven riders. He ain't got much chance of holdin' his own place."

"The sheriff?"

"He says he cain't do nothin' till Colter does somethin'. By then it'll be too late."

"What about selling to someone else?"

"Who? Who wants to buy trouble?"

Adams sipped his coffee and stared off into the distance, silent so long that the others stirred uncomfortably. Finally he said bluntly, "I'll give you twenty-five hundred."

They had expected almost anything but this and gaped at him incredulously. "Wh-what would you want with it?" Oncina asked at last.

"I don't know."

The fast, directness of the statement seemed to convince them. The man looked back at the others questioningly and received a tiny nod from the woman. Half hopefully he said, "With the cattle, it's worth four thousand easy."

"You've already sold it for fifteen hundred."

"Yeah, you're right I reckon. I jist..." Again Oncina let his words trail off hopelessly.

"And it's not worth that if it can't be held."

"Reckon that's true," Oncina said. He looked down at his boots and kicked at a splinter in the floor with his toe, unable to make the decision. It was the woman who finally answered. "It's a fair offer, Mr. Adams." So, calmly, she accepted the inevitable.

"Two more things," Adams said. "Can you be out by Friday?" When the man nodded, he continued, "Is there someone in town to handle the legal end?"

"There's Judge Holman."

Adams knew the Judge worked at home and the

prospect of visiting there was hardly attractive. "No one else?"

"Only Sam Goss, but he's up to Denver jist now."

"It will have to be the Judge then. When's the best

"Can you be there at seven thirty tonight?"

"Sure, fine," Oncina said. "Ah...you ain't foolin me are you? This is really a deal?"

"Juan," his wife chided. "Mr. Adams did not ride all the way out here for a joke."

"It's a deal," Frank said. "One other thing, though. It would be best if as few people as possible heard about this."

"Yeah, sure. I ain't lookin' fer trouble." Realizing how he was obviously running from trouble, Oncina flushed and looked away.

Chapter 6

Adams usually made a habit of promptness. This evening, standing within sight of Judge Holman's home, he watched Oncina drive up on time and still tarried five minutes before approaching the house. Finally he forced himself through the gate and up to the door. He gave the bell knob a hard twist and saw, through the window, a boy get up from his chair to answer the ring. From the other side of the door a woman's voice called, "I'll get it," and the door swung open.

For an instant he thought the woman standing there was the one who had so nearly shot him on the street. He felt a flood of relief when he realized it wasn't. The resemblance was strong; a younger sister he thought. He introduced himself, adding. "I believe Judge Holman is expecting me."

The girl closed the door behind Adams. The boy had come to the parlor entrance. She said, "Glynn, will you tell dad that Mr. Adams is here?"

The boy crossed the hall, knocked on a closed door and received a muffled answer from the other side. He opened the door and, standing one foot with the other waving taillike behind him, leaned as far into the room as his grip on the doorframe allowed to transmit his message.

There were four men in the room when Adams entered. Oncina made the introductions. The Judge got down to business with cool efficiency. "Juan tells me you're buying the Chain Link."

Frank nodded.

"And you want me to draw up the papers?" There was a hint of surprise in the Judge's voice. This was a land where bills of sale and receipts were as often as not scribbled on old envelopes or the sides of flour sacks.

"I don't want there to be any doubt about this. I understand the title is already under a cloud because somebody wouldn't use a lawyer."

"You know about that then?"

"Yes. It doesn't worry me particularly."

"Good," the Judge said, relieved that he would not have to risk the sale by bringing the matter up. "Then we'll get busy. It shouldn't take long."

Their business completed, they moved to the hall and stood there as the Judge bid a final good-by to Oncina. In the parlor someone was playing the piano; a firm, even touch drawing a soft, singing tone from the instrument. Adams glanced in and saw the girl who had admitted him seated at the keyboard of a low, rectangular rosewood piano. The polished

46

surface of the wood, glowing with a deep luster in the yellow lamplight, matched perfectly the dark hair that framed her oval face. He realized that she was looking toward him and framed his lips to say. "Beautiful," without a sound. She accepted the compliment by inclining her head slightly.

The front door was open now, and Oncina had already stepped to the veranda. He could delay no longer. Accepting his hat and the coolly formal, "Good night," from the Judge, he followed the rancher down the steps.

The door closed behind him, but did not shut off the music, which followed him down the path, to linger in his mind far beyond the range of its actual sound.

Back in the hallway, the three men listened to Adams' fading steps and looked at each other questioningly. "Well, what do you make of it?" the Judge asked at last.

"You've got me," Will said. "I can't figure it."

Tom Holman stood twisting his lower lip between thumb and forefinger thoughtfully. "I'd say that Colter threw a boomerang that may just come back and hit him," he said at last. "Adams isn't working for him, that's certain, he's not likely to be paying twenty-five hundred for something he could have for fifteen. That means Adams is doing this on his own."

"But why?" Will asked.

"Maybe he thinks he knows how to hold it. If he does, he has a good buy. Maybe he feels there was an effort to frame him in Tom's killing. It was only luck that he wasn't blamed. If there hadn't been a reliable witness he would have had a hard time convincing anyone he hadn't done it.

"The last seems more reasonable," the Judge said, "he thinks Mark set him up and wants to hit back at him. Mark sent for him, that's sure, then apparently refused to hire him."

"More likely he refused the job. I know something of his reputation. It doesn't seem to fit with what Mark wanted. It could be that he hopes this will help

47

prove it."

"Why ask us not to say anything about it then?" Will asked.

"He probably wants to announce it himself, in his own good time."

There was a pause in their conversation. A voice from from the stairs took advantage of it. "What's a boomerang?"

They looked up to see Glynn perched on the top step,swinging a shoe back and forth by its laces.

"What are you doing there?" the Judge demanded with mock severity.

"Just sittin. What's a boomerang?"

"You're supposed to be getting ready for bed."

"I know. What's a boomerang, Uncle Tom?"

They all laughed, and the boy's uncle explained to an audience which became increasingly sceptical as he went on.

"Ah, you're kiddin' me," the boy said, then threw the shoe into the air behind him and went scrambling after it in an effort to catch it before it hit the floor.

Chapter 7

Adams had discovered that a great deal could be learned about a town just by listening; a talkative barber, a friendly waitress, or a private eavesdropping post such as the one he had found at the end of the balcony above the hotel veranda. Every evening since the shooting; he had sat there in the dark and listened to the conversation float up from below. Among other things, he learned that her name was Ann and that she worked in her uncle's grocery store. This last pleased him, for it meant he would have a chance to

see her again.

To the town, Frank Adams was a cold, unfeeling gunman, his presence tolerated because there was no legal way to remove it. They would have been amazed if they had known that behind this facade was a lonely and unsure man; a man who could look back through a dozen years, recalling a dozen times when an attractive woman had passed casually, fleetingly through his life, yet had attracted him strongly enough to leave a memory so vivid that every feature, every expression was deeply etched in his mind.

Actually these were fantasies rather than memories; the fantasies of a lonley man. Because he knew no way to change it, he had learned to live with loneliness, as a deformed man lives with his deformity, by convincing himself it was unimportant. His subconscious remained unconvinced, seizing fleeting impressions and building fantasies around them. Now it had added this girl to the array.

Having some purchases to make gave him a legitimate excuse to see her at least once more. He stepped through the door of Will Holman's grocery, started to close it, then pulled it open again for the granite faced woman who followed him in. She flicked a pair of icy blue eyes over him and cleared her throat in what might have been a thank you, but probably wasn't.

It was cool and clean smelling inside. The faint odor of spices and freshly ground coffee hung in the air along with the delicate, tangy aroma of dried fruit.

Ann was there, waiting on a round faced, heavy woman in a faded gingham dress. Her uncle was serving the only other customer, a twelve year old girl. Frank felt a surge of disappointment as he saw that the store keeper was almost finished, while Ann was just starting to total her sales.

Will Holman handed her shopping basket to the girl, said "Thank you, Helen," then turned to Adams. "Yes, sir?"

Before Frank could answer, an acid voice behind

50

him said, "Are these the only potatoes you have?"

"Yes, Mrs. Milner," the grocer answered.

"They're soft."

"They're quite good for this time of year."

"Humph. All right, I'll take some. And some coffee and..." Completely ignoring Adams, she rattled off her demands. The grocer hesitated, torn between the waspish, but regular, customer and the probable transient.

"Well?" she demanded impatiently.

Actually pleased, Adams helped him with a faint not toward the woman. Then Ann finished with her customer and said, with a warm smile, "May I help you?"

The smile was natural, and probably impersonal, but to a man accustomed to calculated coolness, it was especially attractive.

He managed a quick, uncertain smile then, to cover his uncertainty, stated his wants so rapidly that she held up her hands against the flow of words.

"Slow down, slow down. Give me a chance."

He repeated the order, and she turned to move along the shelves behind the counter. Her body jerked unevenly as she walked, and he could hear the heavy thumping as an artificially built up shoe struck against the hardwood floor. He felt a momentary sympathy, which gave way quickly to admiration. He felt sure she was untouched by the handicap, there was no resentment, no self pity. "Something else?" she asked, snapping him out of a momentary reverie.

He glanced at the items on the counter and could think of nothing more. "I guess that's it, thank you." He stuffed his purchases into a pair of worn saddlebags.

It was nearly sundown when he rode up to his newly acquired Chain Link. The buildings were still in the sun, but their shadows lay long on the ground. The place was deserted. Everywhere there was evidence of the haste with which it had been left. In the barn, some broken harness hung on the wall.

51

Easily repairable, it had either been overlooked, or left because of lack of room. A pitchfork with a broken tine stood in a corner, beneath a set of metal wheel rims. A bag of nails lay on the ground beside the door, abandoned at the last minute, but seeming to give promise that the owner would be returning.

Frank crossed the yard to the house. There was the same indication of hurried departure here. A battered brass bed stood in one corner of the main room; the mattress gone, the bare springs stretched between the uprights like a huge spider web. To add to the illusion, a single boot lay in its center like a helpless victim entangled in its strands. The floor was strewn with odds and ends of clothing, pieces of paper and bits of broken glass from a smashed mirror.

Adams turned to the kitchen. It faced the west and a bright shaft of yellow sunlight struck, almost horizontally, through the window to float like a bar of gold in the dust filled air; its far end anchored to the square iron stove. He put his hand to the stove, found it still warm, and lifted aside one of the lids. The Oncina's must have left only a short time before, there was still a good bed of coals under the shallow layer of gray-white ash.

Among a few bits of crockery and tinware on the shelf beside the stove were a chipped cup and a battered saucepan. He filled the pan at the well, raided his saddlebags for coffee and returned to the kitchen. He turned the damper in the stove's chimney, opened the door below the grate and set the pan of water among the bright coals. While it was heating, he folded a few coffee beans in a square of cloth and began to pulverize them with the butt of his gun. It wasn't good coffee, but just then it needed only to be hot and strong to taste as if it had been made at Antoine's.

All brightness had gone from the sky by the time he had circled the house and climbed the slope behind it where he spread his blankets for the night.

He spent the next day keeping watch on the house

below, sometimes sitting with his back against the trunk of a quaking aspen, sometimes pacing restlessly up and down. Twice he built a tiny, smokeless fire to cook breakfast and lunch. He was just wondering about supper when they came.

A dozen riders approached the ranch in a loose bunch. They spread out as they hit the yard, coming to a halt in a rough semicircle around the house. Frank watched with a professional eye as half of them swung down and moved to investigate the buildings, returning a minute later with their report. He felt no surprise as they began tearing apart a haystack and piling the hay against the walls of buildings. The still mounted men threw their ropes over anything they could pull down, corral posts, front gate, well housing, and dragged them over to the barn. They were thorough about it. There was to be nothing left of the Chain Link. Finally the torches were lit and they moved like fireflies around the yard.

Adams waited until they had remounted and started toward town, then mounted his own horse and rode through the timber to the crest of the ridge. He struck a narrow trail that dropped down to the main road. By pushing his horse he reached the road five minutes ahead of the J.C. and had increased this to fifteen by the time he reached town.

He didn't need the extra time. He found Mark Colter where he expected to; at a poker table in the Staghorn. This was a regular Saturday night game, with virtually the same players participating. Their regular table was on a raised platform, once the stage, at the rear of the barroom. This had been made into a semi-private card room by the addition of three steps at the center, with a low partition, topped by a two foot green curtain, on each side. The arrangement had the advantage of easy service from the bar; simply by lifting a hand above the curtain, a player could summon drinks, cigars, or cards, while a degree of privacy was maintained by an unwritten rule that nobody went up the steps unless there was a chair open.

Somehow no one felt like mentioning the rule when Adams took his beer from the bar, climbed the steps and stood at a discreet distance from the table to wach the game. It was straight five card stud. He watched two rounds before Dutcher and two other J.C. hands pushed through the front door and began weaving their way through the crowd.

Mark saw them coming, said, "Deal me out," and went to the bottom of the stairs to meet them, giving Adams a curious stare as he passed. Frank watched another deal, then drifted over to the steps. He leaned against the end of the partition a half dozen feet from where Mark was talking to Ben. He waited until Mark turned back toward the table, then said, challengingly, "These your men, Colter?"

Silence started there and swept across the room like a wave. The suddenness of the challenge caught Mark off guard. His slight nod was entirely subconscious as he tried to order his thoughts. Frank gave him no time. "You give them their orders?" There was no nod this time, but Adams continued as though there had been. "Then you're responsible for what they do."

"What are you getting at?" Mark asked uncertainly.

"They just burned out the Chain Link."

It set Mark back on his heels. The men who had done the job had just gotten here, yet Adams, who had been standing watching the game, knew all about it. It was impossible. His answer, when it came, was an inadquate, "What's that to you?"

"It was my place. I bought it two days ago." It was another shock. Mark just gaped at him as he went on, "The place may have looked deserted, but that gave you no right to burn it. It was a mistake. About a thousand dollars worth of mistake. At least that's my price and I don't intend to bargain."

The cards were on the table. The next move was Mark's. He could pay; a thousand dollars with nothing to show for it, backing down in front of the men who had watched him ride around like an empire builder

54

for months, or he could fight. He wondered with a sudden fear, whether he was expected to fight; whether it had been planned that way so that Adams could kill him and end this fight as he had ended others. But with the odds four to one? Involuntarily he glanced around at the three men with him.

Adams said, his voice so soft that only the four of them could hear, "They're not here, just the two of us." His meaning was clear. Regardless of who made the first move, Colter would be the target. And Adam's reputation said that he would not only get Colter but that man who moved first.

Colter hesitated, his mouth dry, chilled fingers still playing along his back. He couldn't fight; he didn't want to back down. Was there anything else? Could he just say, "That's your tough luck," turn and walk out? It would still be backing down, Adams stood between him and the poker game, but it wouldn't look so bad. Would it work? If Adams made a quick move, could he depend on the others to hold firm? The answer to that question killed his idea. Dutcher would hold, the others, their nerves drawn tight, would go for their guns at the first sign of trouble. He was suddenly sorry they were here.

Of the four men, only Dutcher managed to view the scene with any degree of objectivity. The result was a grudging admiration for Adams. "A real professional," he thought. The thing had been handled perfectly. The choice of words, the way they had been used and, above all, his position.

He was well above them and had only to drop to his knee to be behind the partition. This might not protect him, although the hard wood corner post might turn a bullet, but it would make him a difficult target, while they were grouped out in the open without cover. Considering that he was good enough to get in the first two shots, Ben concluded that the odds were not as long as they seemed. Mark had reached the same conclusion. He had his share of courage normally, but this had come too suddenly. He never had a chance to get himself set. He moistened dry lips and said, as steadily as possible, "Maybe we were in too much of a hurry. You prove you own the place and I'll pay for the damages."

A whisper of sound crossed the room. The men behind Colter let their weight drop back into their chairs. Adams reached into his pocket and pulled out the bill of sale. Colter gave it one quick look and handed it back. "All right," he said.

Chapter 8

The incident put Mark in a black mood which was still with him the next morning, making his normally dark features seem even darker. There were two men in his office; Ben Dutcher, half seated on the corner of the desk and Hippo Krale, sprawled in a big, hide covered chair in the corner.

The nickname of "Hippo" (inevitable as a red haired man's "Red") was an unkind reference to his grotesque pearshaped body. The sharply sloping shoulders and narrow chest seemed determined to emphasize the hugeness of the lower body; an unnecessary determination, for even Dutcher's broad chest would not have minimized the ungainly, bulky hips and buttocks and tremendous thighs. His face continued the poor proportioning. The forehead and eyes were too large, while the mouth was small and the jaw narrow.

"What does he want?" It was Dutcher who asked.

"Money," Mark answered, his voice surly. "What does his kind always want"

Hippo nodded, "He sure ain't the kind to take up ranchin', that's for sure. Least ways not on a one man spread like the Chain Link." He finished filling his pipe and set the stem between teeth so white, so even, so perfect they were an insult to the rest of his face.

"That's right," Mark said. "He's out for a quick dollar. That's what he came here for, then for some reason, he turned the job down."

"What reason did he give?" Ben asked.

Mark snorted. "Claimed he didn't work undercover. Said when he rode for an outfit he didn't hide it."

"Moral bastard for a hired gun, ain't he?" Hippo said. "Maybe we should issue uniforms like the army."

To Dutcher the arguement seemed reasonable, but he said only, "It didn't matter. The town knew he had been out here before he even got back."

"They wouldn't have if he had gone on to Hortonville then rode back like he was supposed to," Colter said with annoyance. "Anyway he turned the job down, but he still wants the money. I guess he figures he can blackmail me into giving it to him to get the Chain link."

"Are you going to?" Ben asked.

"What do you think?"

Mark's answer was not a question, but Ben took it as such. "I think you should," he said.

The others looked at him in surprise and Hippo sneered, "What's the matter, Ben, you scared of him?"

Ben brushed the question aside with an annoyed

wave of his hand. "Don't talk like a fool. Adams is a damn tough man, he proved that last night, and he could be just as dangerous to us as Pierce was."

"Hell, Pierce had a crew behind him," Hippo grunted. "Adams is just one man. He may be greased lightenin' with a gun, but he's still only one man. We could send a couple of men into town some night and he'd never know what hit him. Don't think the town would give a damn about him, either."

"They wouldn't care about him," Colter agreed, "but they still do about Pierce. A lot of people have us pegged for that, but at least they aren't sure. They will be, though, if Adams gets it the same way. There's too many men in town that I need to let it get away from me. Now a gun fight like I wanted with Pierce would still be all right. If you'd like to ride in and call him on the street..." he let his voice trail off into a malice filled laugh.

"Hell, he'd put three holes into me before I got my gun clear," Hippo said with unexpected candor.

"Then we've got to think of something else."

Dutcher said, "Buy the place from him. With him and Pierce out of the way, there's nobody to worry about. You would have tried to buy Pierce off if you thought there was a chance. Why not Adams?"

Colter thought it over through a long moment of silence. "You got a point there," he conceded.

Hippo shrugged elaborately. "It's your money. I just can't see all this worry about one man. Nobody's likely to hire him, and what can he do alone?"

Ben said, voice slightly sarcastic, "I wouldn't have thought yesterday that he could have a thousand dollars of Mark's money today. That's the trouble, you can't figure him. The others, yes, but not him. With him around you're likely to run into something like last night at any time. He probably doesn't figure on a big profit, maybe a thousand. Figure he paid two, you're still getting a pretty good buy."

"Yeah, only twice what I could have had it for."

"A drop in the bucket in the long run, Mark."

Mark considered it for a minute. "All right," he said. "We'll give him his profit. Take a couple of men and ride in to see him. Try to get it for less, but you can go as high as twenty-five. With the thousand he's alredy got, that should be enough."

"And if it isn't?"

"That's what you're taking the men for, to help him change his mind. No guns, understand, just wait your chance, then work him over. Do a good job. Let him know we aren't fooling. If he happens to get his gun hand stepped on, that's his tough luck." The events of the preceding night still rankled him. Colter took a malicious pleasure in issuing this order, even to the point of half hoping Adams would refuse to sell.

'I've got a job for you, too, Hippo," he continued.

Hippo pushed the third of a series of smoke rings through the still air, gave a short, self approving laugh as it passed cleanly through the other two, then said, "Yeah?"

"Yeah. I want you to gather a couple hundred head and drive them over to the east side of Turtle Back Ridge."

"That's Martinson's range," Hippo said unnecessarily.

"It's free range. I've decided to use it."

"Think he'll let you get away with it?"

"If he's smart he will, but he's not; just stubborn. Anyway he'll figure if he lets us get away with this, we'll hit him somewhere else, and he'd be right. If I know him, he'll come storming over there with his whole crew to throw you off."

"He'll find that tougher than he thinks," Hippo said.

"No," Mark corrected, "easier. I want him to run you off, but in my way. Knowing Dave, I think it'll work. You move into that line shack up there with a couple of men. Post a couple more where they can watch the Lazy M and see which the old boy jumps. Meanwhile I'll arrange to have him find out about it almost before you get there. That way he'll have every reason to expect to catch you by surprise if he moves fast.

Chances are he'll circle and come over the ridge, in which case he'll only be a couple of hundred yards away when you see him.

"Then again he may ride straight up the valley. In that case you be so busy on the other side of the shack, fixing the corral or something, that they can get close before you see them. Either way you let them get up close before you make a break for your rifles. They won't want any serious shooting, so they'll drop a few shots into the dust between you and your rifles to keep you away from them."

"Seems to me you're doin' a lot of guessin' about what they're goin' to do," Hippo said.

"Sure I am. They might not come at all, but I'll give ten to one they do, and I'll give the same odds it's the way I said, because I know how they think, and they don't have a lot of choices. If I'm wrong we don't lose anything."

"You don't," Hippo said. "What makes you so sure they won't be shootin' for keeps?"

"They won't. But if you don't believe it, I'll let someone else do the job."

"Oh, I'll do it," Hippo said. "I just think you're goin' at it wrong. Why not have the crew lined up behind the ridge, and when they come in shootin' you drop down and finish them?"

Colter heaved an exasperated sigh. "Because I want them to start things. And I want to establish that they did, before we do anything. Then whatever we do is a reprisal. Anyway it wouldn't work. They aren't so dumb they wouldn't check that ridge."

"Maybe, but do you think anybody'll swallow that reprisal stuff? Hell, they'll know you baited him."

"Sure. But how many times has somebody been baited into a gunfight and killed? And what's it called? Self defence!"

"Maybe," Hippo said again. "I think you're too damn worried about the town. When you own this end of the valley, they'll be fallin' all over themselves to lick lyour boots."

61

"Some of them. Maybe all, if we don't push them too far. They're not a one horse, scared-of-their-own-shadow town, though, and they don't need me any more that I need them. That's why I want to keep this out of town. That and the sheriff. I can handle him, but I don't own him. I have to give him some reason to look the other way. If enough people are saying that the damn fool only got what he asked for, that will do it. So this has to look as good as you can make it."

Hippo nodded slowly and Colter continued," After they take over, you have to see to it they rough you up. There will be a fifty dollar bonus in it," he added quickly, squelching Hippo's budding objection. "You start a fight and take a whipping. If it isn't bad enough, have one of the boys improve on it afterward. That'll give you a good reason to go into town to see the Doc. Then you talk it up over a couple of drinks. Lay it on thick. It would be even better if we got somebody shot, but I'm afraid I'm not paying enough to get any volunteers for that." He laughed at his own joke, drawing a chuckle from Ben and a hearty guffaw from Hippo.

Chapter 9

Dutcher had been wrong in thinking that Adams was out for a quick profit. He had merely planned to publicly set himself against Colter, make certain everyone knew it, then sell out, hopefully leaving the impression that he had never been connected with Colter, so he wouldn't have had anything to do with Pierce's death. Having accomplished this, he didn't know why, when Dutcher brought the expected offer, he refused it.

He had no idea what he intended to do with the

place and was wondering about it as he strolled down State Street in the late afternoon. It wasn't his preoccupation with this, though, that made him miss the danger in the man on the walk ahead. It was the skill with which the man dissembled it. He was leaning with his left elbow against a roof support at shoulder height, the picture of indolent unconcern; and he was unarmed. As Frank approached, he brought his right hand casually to his mouth with a lighted cigarette. Instead of drawing on the smoke, he said, almost conversationally, "Better hold it right there, there's a pair of scatterguns centered on your belt buckle from the alley."

Without losing sight of the man, Adams stopped and wheeled around to face the alley. Ben Dutcher was there and a stranger. Both were covering him with shotguns.

Dutcher said, "This way and don't make any quick moves." The man on the walk retrieved a rifle from a doorway and followed Frank down the alley.

He murmured, "Careful," as Adams passed between the two shotguns, reading his thoughts. Then they were in the area behind Will Holman's store.

There was a small, square yard of hard packed dirt, enclosed on three sides by the now empty buildings. On the fourth side was a five foot fence with a gate and a well worn path leading to a pair of privies. Beyond that; a broad, open field, its tall grass swaying laxily in the breeze. Although only half a block from State Street, it was an isolated spot. Nodding at Adams' gunbelt, Dutcher said, "Take it off, with your left hand." Frank unbuckled the belt and held it until Ben indicated the loading platform at the store's rear door. Frank put it on the floor and, in response to another order, slid it across to the door.

Dutcher unbuckled his own gun, handing it to one of his companies. "Stay out of this," he said.

He was being given a chance, Frank thought wryly. Better make the most of it. As Ben stepped close, he

64

leaped forward taking him by surprise and landing two solid blows. Not solid enough. As he tried to dance away, a fist like a club caught him on the side of the head, spinning him around and dropping him to his knees. He dived away and scrambled to his feet, but with amazing speed, Ben caught him before he could turn completely and slammed him back against a building wall. He hung there a moment as though dazed then, as Ben came in close, ducked under a jabbing left and put all the strength and weight of his body behind a desperate right under the heart. He felt the numbing shock the full length of his arm, but it didn't stop the big man. He knew then that he could break his hands on this rock of a man and never hurt him.

They were almost the same height, but Dutcher carried an extra forty pounds, most of it in the raw power of chest and shoulder. Perhaps it was this power that led Ben into his first mistake. He reached out to sweep the gunman up in his arms, and for a second he was off balance. Sensing it, Frank stepped close, twisting until his hip was against the other's waist and his arm around it. He let Ben's weight come forward across him, then gave a sudden upward snap with his hip that sommersaulted Ben to the ground. It was a wicked hip throw that hurt the bigger man for the first time. He thought he saw his chance then and drove down at the prone figure with his knees. Again Dutcher was too quick for him. His knees hit the ground instead, sending him sprawling across Ben's back. He managed to hook an arm under Dutcher's chin and, a second later, scissored his legs around Ben's. For a minute he was in the saddle.

Staying behind, out of reach of those piledriver fists, he rode him as he might a wild horse. Each time Ben pushed himself up with his arms, Frank knocked one of them out from under him, driving him back into the dust. When Ben did manage to struggle to his feet, Adams hooked an ankle, dropping him down again, and always he clung like a burr to his back. He couldn't hurt the man this way, but he could make him use up his magnificent strength carrying the double weight; postponing the inevitable in the hope that something might happen.

There was too much strength in Ben. With a virtual explosion of speed and power, he shook Adams loose and dragged him around, pinning one arm to his side. Adams felt the crushing power of that grip and knew he had only seconds before his breath would be driven from him and, possibly, his ribs broken. He almost wasted them in a moment of panic, striking futilely at Ben's head with his free hand. Reason returned and he raked Ben's face with his fingers, trying for the eyes; when Ben jerked his head back, dropped his weight in a twisting motion against the uncircling arms, he used his slenderness to literally eel out of the grip.

Then he was on his knees in front of an off balance form. Reaching out, he caught Ben's ankle with one hand and drove the other forearm against Ben's knee. Again Ben was thrown heavily, and again Frank tried to leap on his back as he came to his feet. He missed. A backhand blow caught him on the side of the head, and suddenly he was in the dirt with ears ringing and the salty taste of blood in his mouth.

His eyes refused to focus, but they did see the shadow which passed across them and he braced himself as a weight like a falling horse landed on him. Reaching out blindly to grab something, he caught Ben's wrist and clung desperately. He never remembered circling Ben's arm and catching his own wrist with his other hand but, without knowing how, he had the double wrist lock. He hooked Ben's ankle with his foot then, bridging, used all his waning strength to force the other's arm up behind his back. It was calculated to break an arm. That it didn't testified to the iron there. Its failure ended Adams' chances.

An involuntary cry of pain was forced past Dutcher's lips but, like a wounded bear, the injury only made him more dangerous. He shook himself free and they both came to their feet. Noticing his slowness, Frank tried to bring him down again by diving at his legs. He had been slowed even more than Ben, who stepped quickly to one side and, using the side of his fist as though it were a club, smashed Adams down into the dirt.

With the same hand he grabbed Adams by his shirt and hauled him to his feet. Ignoring the pain in his shoulder, he swung a vicious right to the jaw. It ended the fight there, Adams was out on his feet and would not have even been on his feet except that the blow sent him staggering back into the arms of one of the onlookers who, almost in self defense, grabbed him.

In his anger, Ben could only see that he was still standing. A man whom he should have been able to snap like a twig. Anger blinded him to everything but the need to beat the man down. He stepped forward and struck twice, once with each hand. Frank's body rolled slackly, but did not fall. Dutcher didn't notice the reason and wouldn't have cared if he had. He drew back his fist for a third blow when something else impinged on his consciousness, arresting his hand in mid air. It was voice from the doorway of the store that called shrilly, "Stop it. Stop it."

Turning, he looked up and saw Ann Holman. Oddly his first thought was not to wonder how she happened to be there, or even to consider Adams' gun, held uncertainly in both hands, but rather to think how attractive she looked standing there. Damn near as pretty as her sister, he thought. It wasn't the first time he had oticed. Behind him one of his men, less concerned with beauty than business, called, "She cain't hit nothin' with that."

Her answering voice had lost its edge of hysteria and was quite calm now. "I don't have to," she said. "I only have to shoot to bring a dozen men. And I would only have to tell them he was trying to protect me from you."

It wasn't the threat that stopped Ben. His anger had

died as quickly as it had been born so that now he almost welcomed the interruption.

Reaching down, he picked up his hat, beat it against his thigh several times, donned it and lifted his hand to its brim in a salute without mockery. Over his shoulder he called, "Let's go," and moved toward the alley.

His companions fell in behind him, the one who had been holding Adams giving him a parting shove back against the fence where he hung, half sitting, half standing, feet apart, palms pressed against the boards. Glancing back, Dutcher saw him there and muttered, "Tougher than he looks."

Chapter 10

When they had gone, Ann lowered the heavy pistol and limped down the ramp and across the yard. To Frank she was a vague, uncertain figure, constantly jumping in and out of focus. He had only a dreamer's memory of getting to the store. It seemed that he suddenly possessed some strange magic so that by mental powers alone he could rise from the ground and dirft slowly forward. Occasionally this power would run low and he would drop down until his feet pushed the ground, but each time he drew a fresh measure of this strange power and floated on, up the ramp, across the platform, into the store.

The world ahead of him seemed to have caught fire. Small at first, it grew and spread and suddenly a part of it leaped across the distance to catch and grow and throw out its blazing sparks in turn. His stomach twisted into knots around the lead weight already there. Perspiration broke from every pore and ran down his body until his shirt was soaked and his face glistened. His hands trembled as he tried to push himself away from the blaze.

He actually managed to shove himself back a foot before his vision cleared, and the fire became the glow of an oil lamp on the table in front of him; the sparks, reflections from its cut crystal base. Beyond the table the distant fire resolved itself into the separate flames of a tiny, two burner oil stove set against the rear wall.

Ann was standing by the stove, dipping a cloth into a shallow pan on one of the burners. She half turned when she heard him try to push away from the table. Now she turned fully, bringing the pan of water to the table. He had never been completely unconscious, but he must have been on the edge for a long time, the water was steaming hot. He felt something trickle down the side of his cheek and lifted his hand to it.

"Better not touch it," she warned.

He tried to moisten his lips with his tongue, but found it as dry as they were. It took three tries before he could speak. "Do I look as bad as I feel?" His voice was a husky whisper.

"Just about, I'm afraid," she answered with a small smile. "I'll be able to tell better when I get some of the dirt off." She wrung the cloth out and began to wash the blood and dirt from his face. Her hands were gentle, although whatever she had put into the water smarted wickedly, and her voice was pleasantly soft; the perfect therapy for his jumpy nerves. Apparently she realized this for she continued to talk as she worked. "Except for this cut on your cheek, there doesn't seem to be any serious damage. It should have a stitch or two, but I'm afraid it will have to wait until the doctor returns."

"You're a good nurse."

"Thank you. As long as I can remember my sister and I dreamed of becoming Florence Nightengales. Margaret was almost Dan Prentis' official nurse. Then, when she decided to marry Jim, I started to help him. I'm not as good as she is, though. Mostly I help out with babies, or tie up cut fingers. You're my first

70

real battle casualty. I'm glad I happened by."

"Happy to be of service." He was a man who rarely joked and was pleased by her quick laughter.

"I'm sure you planned it that way."

"Of course, what else?" he said. "How did you happen to be here on a Sunday?"

"Ice cream."

He said, "Huh?" through teeth clenched against the bite of an iodine soaked swab.

"My brother, Glynn, is crazy about ice cream. Somehow he managed to wrangle a piece of ice from Ed Sauer. It must have taken some doing because Ed isn't noted for generosity. I promised to make some ice cream with it, then after he and Dad had gone for it, I found we were out of salt. So I came to get some. Luckily we keep it back here." She gestured toward a shelf where several sacks of rock salt stood, one pulled to the edge. "I was just getting one down when I heard the noise out back and saw the fight from the window."

"And you went out and stopped it?"

"Hardly that. I'm afraid it was pretty well over when I made my entrance." She crossed to the stove and lifted the lid from a pot. The rich aroma of brewing coffee filled the room. Here was a real woman, he thought admiringly. With him sitting there half unconscious and bleeding, she had thought to put on the coffee pot.

As she was settling the grounds with an egg, he tried to remember the fight's aftermath, but could recall only that hazy impression of drifting through space.

"How did I get here?"

"You were still on your feet, and I helped you some."

"Some! You must have half carried me. With your bad foot you shouldn't have done it. You might have hurt yourself."

"I'm stronger than I look," she said. She was surprised at the casual reference to her infirmity, but

71

pleased, also. It was a refreshing change from the scrupulously careful avoidance of the subject. She set a cup before him, filling it halfway, and said, "Try a little of that. Maybe it'll help."

He lifted the cup, using both hands to keep from slopping it over himself, and drained half of it in one gulp. The lead weight in his stomach simply raised up, turned over, and settled down again. He grimaced as it did.

"I guess I should have made tea," she said apologetically. "It might have been better for you."

"Glad you didn't. I detest it." He managed another fleeting smile as he pushed the cup toward her suggestively. This time he was able to pick it up with one hand.

She said abruptly, "What will you do about this?"

"Do?" His eyebrows arched in surprise. "Why nothing. What did you expect me to do?"

"I don't know. I thought..." she flushed and looked down at the table.

"That I'd go out and shoot him down the first chance I got? My reputation must be worse than I thought."

"Well, everyone says you came here to shoot Jim Pierce." Her tone was defensive, but her questioning look showed that she had reserved judgement.

He shook his head. "That's what I was sent for. I didn't know that until I got here, didn't like it when I found out." Normally he would have let this statement suffice. Somehow it had become important that she understand.

"Fighting is all I know, all I'm any good at." The pain in his battered face reminded him to qualify that. "Not with my fists, though," he added with a wry smile. "I was deputy sheriff at Hays City for a while and marshal at Two Rivers. I rode shotgun down on the Overland and ran guns across the border to one of those two bit Mexican revolutions.

"Then there were special jobs for small outfits whose regular crew couldn't handle them. Someone had put up a dam and cut off their water, or they were being rustled blind and the law couldn't do anything. Maybe a mining claim was jumped, or a mine was having trouble getting its ore out. And, of course, I was involved in a couple of range wars. I won't say everything I did was always legal, but I always thought it was right. Reputations, though, are based on results, not on the right or wrong of them. It was my reputation that Colter sent for.

"I was born a hundred years too late. I think of myself as a professional soldier. As a youngster I read all the romantic novels glorifying him. Then I tried to live the role only to find it had gone out of style."

"Perhaps we're more civilized now."

"Are we? I don't think so. We still hire killers to go out and kill for us. We just don't glorify it, we rationalize it; call it by a different name. We put a badge on a killer and call it law enforcement." Seeing her instant objection, he added quickly, "I'm not saying lawmen are all hired killers. On the contrary, few of them are. It's just that when a town has a tough problem, instead of hiring a good lawman and backing him to the hilt, it hires a tough one and then stands aside, closing its eyes to what he is, or how he works. If they're lucky they get somebody like Tom Smith or Bill Tilghman. If they're not, they get somebody like Jeb Treach, over at Evensville. He enjoys killing and a badge is a license to do it. But as long as he gets the job done everyone pats him on the back and says how great he is."

"They don't necessarily approve, Mr. Adams. Father says that a community must give its lawmen its support and confidence, or his hands are tied."

"True. One or two times they have to assume a killing could not be avoided. Not eight times, though. That's Jeb's record in Evensville, unless he's added to it since I last heard. Of course they were all outsiders, so Evensville boasts about how he handles troublemakers and drifters. He's never brought back a fugitive alive, even when it was known he was

73

unarmed. The town doesn't see anything wrong. "Makes the crooks think twice about anything in our town." Adams let his voice become nasal and whiney in imitation of some remembered townsman. "They'll get fed up with him eventually, but right now he's well liked. There's hardly a person there who wouldn't welcome him into his home."

"I wouldn't," Ann said firmly. "Not someone as cruelly callous as that. I don't think this town would accept a man like that either."

"Maybe not. Yet even a town like this hires killing in one way or another. If it isn't howling for the army to kill off all the Indians to, quote, 'make the country safe for decent folk,' it's putting up reward posters like the one across the street. Boy named Will Jones, wanted for robbery, three hundred dollars reward— dead or alive. With that poster they've hired a hundred killers to go out and shoot him. Yet he hasn't even been tried yet; legally that is. They tried and sentenced him when they printed it. Have you ever heard anyone protest that kind of poster? Of course not."

"Oh, but I have. Dad is very strongly opposed. He belives a federal judge should have to approve every one of them."

His smile became a chuckle. "Score one for you," he said.

"No, you're right. Dad is the only one who seems to think that way. Even Uncle Will says that if a person is running from the law it's his own fault if he's killed, he should go back and take his medicine."

"If he can get back before he's killed," Frank said. "Maybe your uncle's right. Maybe it's all right to pay three hundred dollars to have him killed. Maybe it's all right to make killing him more attractive to the bounty hunter than bringing him in alive. I don't know. I wonder, though, how they can be so self righteous about hiring the killing and so scornful of the man who earns their pay—unless he's their local lawman, that is. I brought in a man once. He had been

74

convicted of murder and had killed a guard in escaping. But when I took him into town you would have thought he had been a favorite son, while I was the forerunner of the plague. Do you know the strangest thing about it, though?"

"What?"

He did not answer for a moment. When he did it was as if he was trying to convince himself that it had actually occurred. "That town was literally plastered with reward posters—on men wanted in other towns."

There was a sound at the front door, and a voice called questioningly, "Ann?"

"Back here, Dad," she answered.

Footsteps crossed the main store, and the Judge appeared in the doorway stopping abruptly as he saw Adams. He took in the situation at a glance and said, "Trouble?"

"A little discussion about real estate," Frank said dryly.

"Colter?"

"Dutcher."

"Yes, it would be. He's Mark's most active real estate agent," the Judge said lightly, taking his cue from Frank. He wasn't anxious to prolong the conversation, however, and turned to Ann. "The ice is at the house. We better get the salt back there before it melts."

"On the shelf beside the stove," she said. "I had better lock the back door." She moved toward it. There was the sharp click of the bolt sliding home, then her voice again as she said, "Won't you join us later for some ice cream, Mr. Adams?"

Her move to the door had put both her and her father behind Adams, who was reaching across the table for his hat, but directly in front of him was the crystal lamp, each facet of its octagonal base a miniature mirror. Each of the three people in the room was perfectly mirrored in one of them. He could see his own face, its astonishment patent, and

75

he could see the other two, not looking at him, but at each other. The Judge's expression was one of shocked incredulity, almost comic opera in its open-mouthed amazement and strong disapproval, Ann's, a quiet plea for understanding and tolerance.

Because he would do more for this daughter than perhaps anyone else in the world, the Judge gave in with a helpless shrug and repeated her invitation, managing to infuse the words with a measure of welcome.

Even feeling as he did, Adams found the invitation tempting because he wanted to see Ann again. Visualizing an hour of mutual discomfort, he decided against it. "I'm afraid I'm not up to it just now, thank you. It will be about all I can do to get back to the hotel."

"Of course," the Judge said, not quite hiding his relief as he quickly closed the door Ann had so imprudently opened. "We should have realized. Any way I can help?"

"No thank you, I can manage."

"Perhaps some other time," Ann said, deliberately extending the invitation in spite of her father's disapproving frown.

Chapter 11

It was a long time before Adams fell asleep that night. Even when he did, he slept fitfully, dreaming and waking and dreaming again. Ann was in all those dreams, her quiet beauty stirring his desires and accenting his loneliness. At times she seemed to drift toward him, smiling, reaching out. Yet whenever he tried to get closer, someone always moved between them.

The gray light of early dawn was beginning to define the room's windows when exhaustion dropped him into a drugged sleep that lasted until noon. It was three before he eased his aching body down the stairs to the lobby. The desk clerk eyed his battered face slyly, but said nothing. He had shaved, in spite of the pain it cost him, and replaced the bandage on his cheek with a smaller one. There was nothing he could do about a black eye and a huge purple bruise running along the side of his jaw.

He decided the cut on his cheek was the first order of business and turned down State Street toward Dr. Prentis' place. There was no answer to his knock and he was turning away when a voice at his right said, "He ain't here."

Looking around, he saw a boy of about thirteen staring at his bruised face with a frank curiosity far more honest than that of his elders. Evidently he had come from the general store to sweep the walk, he was leaning on a broom as he talked.

"You lose?" he asked, unabashed.

"Afraid so."

"Thought so," the boy said. He jerked his thumb toward the Doctor's office. "He won't get back till near six."

"I guess I better come back then."

"He won't be here."

"Oh?"

"Naw. If'n he's back, he'll be over to the Nugget or at the Chuck Wagon." The boy used his broom handle to indicate the two places, leveling it at his hip like a rifle as he swung it back and forth. "He al'ays has a drink at the Nugget 'fore he eats," he said. "Jist one," he added, proud of his knowledge of the town. "Then he eats over at the Wagon."

Adams covered a smile and asked, "And what does he have to eat?" He was always more at ease with young people.

Instantly the boy rose to the challenge. "Us'lly he has roast beef an' home fries, but on Sunday's he..."

Frank stopped him with a sign of surrender, "All right, you win," he laughed. He started to turn away

78

when the boy, emboldened by the friendliness of the conversation, said abruptly, "You really kill forty men?" The suddenness of the question left Adams speechless and he merely stared until the boy began to shift nervously. Finally he said, "No, son, not nearly that many, and I hope to God I never do."

The question, and the budding hero worship behind it, washed out the momentary pleasure the encounter had given him. His mind returned to his attempt to explain himself to Ann. He was not satisfied with that conversation now. A dozen things came to mind that he wished he had said, and others which he might have said better. It seemed, in fact, as though he had fumbled his chance. Yet he must have gotten through to her a little. She had risked her father's certain disapproval by inviting him to her home only minutes after she had said, so positively, that she would not welcome someone like Jeb Treach. It meant that she had seen a difference even if her father probably would not. The thought lifted his spirits.

In spite of the nearness to dinner time, there were more people on the street now than there had been earlier. More than a dozen moved along the sidewalks or stood in the fading warmth of the sun chatting with friends. A light carriage swung briskly past him as he turned into State Street again, and a buckboard was just pulling away from the general store. Acros the latter he could see that the window of the Doctor's office was dark.

He was wondering whether he should try the Nugget, when he saw four men step from the alley beside the office and head for the saloon. Recognizing Dan Prentis among them, Frank turned that way also. The double doors were still swinging as he reached them and pushed into the barroom. The four men had reached the bar and the barman, deserting a customer at the other end, came down to them. With one hand he swept up the Doctor's bag and set it on the backbar, while with the other he delved beneath the bar to produce a bottle of quality bourbon and four glasses.

Two men left a nearby table to join them, and they formed a tight semicircle at the middle of the bar. Frank decided to have a beer while waiting and ordered one with the standard pantomime. The barman slide it down to him, then turned back to the others and said, "You fellows go over to the lake?"

"Sure did," one of them answered.

"How was the water?"

There was a suspicious quickness with which the Doctor's companions chorused, "Fine. Great. Warm as soup." They looked at Prentis, grinning.

With an entirely serious expression, he asked, "Then what made you all turn blue? Don't tell me it was a royal blood line finally showing up."

"Ach, you're jist gittin' soft, Doc," one of them jeered. Turning to the barman, he added, "He wouldn' go in. Claimed the water was too cold. Why it was jist right, weren't it, Joe?"

"Sure was. Wouldn't have wanted it any warmer," Joe answered. "Doc's had too much easy livin', that's all."

"Maybe," Prentis said. "I sure was softer than you today. You were stiff as an icicle, even crackled when you walked. One good slap on the back, and you would have broken into a thousand pieces. And speaking of noise, Bill, here, must have lost ten years chewing from his teeth. They sounded like a pair of castanets at a Mexican fiesta."

"Why don't y' admit it Doc," Bill said. "You're gettin' old. Y' used to be the first man in every spring. Now y' got to sit by and let us young folks take over."

"I may be getting older, but I'm getting smarter, too. I know potential business when I see it. With half a dozen of you freezing your guts up there, I can figure on four or five bad colds and, with any luck, two or three will turn into pneumonia. With that kind of business staring me in the face, I can't afford to take any chances with myself."

The friendly argument continued, with Prentis

more than holding his own in spite of the odds. Adams attention was drawn to the door as a medium tall, stockily built man shouldered through and walked with a firm, almost aggressively sure step to a place at the bar a few feet from him.

The bartender broke away from the others and came over to greet him warmly. "Anything new at the Lazy M?"

It was spoken casually, but he seemed relieved when the other said, "Nothing out of the ordinary."

The exchange marked the newcomer as the Lazy M owner, Dave Martinson. Recognition crystallized an idea that had been playing around the corners of Frank's mind.

When the barman moved away, Frank decided he would never have a better opportunity to act on it. "You're Dave Martinson?"

The older man turned to stare at him for several seconds before giving a sharp nod.

"I'm Frank Adams." There was another nod. "You've heard that I bought out the Chain Link?"

"So I heard." Martinson's voice was neutral. If he showed none of the welcome he might have for a new neighbor, neither did he show hostility.

"I'd like a word with you if you can spare a minute."

While the rancher could think of nothing they might have to discuss, he was fond of saying that it cost nothing to listen. He gestured toward the door connecting this room with the restaurant next door. "I'm about to have supper. We can talk while we eat if you like."

He led the way through the restaurant to a table in the far rear corner where they would be least noticeable. Clearly he did not care to be seen with the gunman. It annoyed Adams, but he hid his feelings as the rancher gave his order to the waitress then said, "All right."

For the second time in two days, Adams was in the position of wanting to explain himself. He had found it unexpectedly easy to talk to Ann. It would be harder now. Martinson was a blunt man. He would expect a reasonable degree of directness. Yet the chances of his idea being considered were too slm not to set the stage a little. He said, "Colter sent for me. I didn't know what the job was, but had heard rumors of a range war and that sort of thing is my business. I'm not proud of it, I'm not ashamed of it. I won't pretend I see myself as a knight in shining armor, but I do expect my man to have a fair share of justice on his side, and what he wants of me is legitimate. Colter missed on both counts.'

The coffee he had ordered arrived. He was silent as he stirred in a spoonful of sugar, hoping for an indication of what his audience was thinking. He could tell nothing from the craggy face, but decided curiosity would hold him for a while. "I guess anyone with a reputation like mine isn't expected to have any principles. Colter doesn't think so. He made an offer I couldn't accept. When I refused, he just raised his price as if that could be my only objection. It wasn't. I have no price for killing, and I had no connection with that one in any way." He looked straight at Martinson, who accepted the statement with another of his short nods.

"After I turned down the job, I had every intention of heading south again, even got as far as the station."

"What stopped you?" Martinson's tone was frankly curious.

"I don't know. I don't even know why I bought the Chain Link. Not for money certainly Everything considered, I paid a fair enough price for it. I guess I had some idea of showing that I wasn't connected with Colter by making him pay considerably more for the place than he would have had to otherwise."

"That's what that play Saturday night was all about? Damn dangerous way to get attention."

Adams smiled thinly. "Not really. None of them is the kind to risk his neck without orders, and Mark wasn't likely to give the orders. Not just then, anyway."

"So he made you an offer?" Martinson asked. It was Adams' turn to nod. "Not enough?"

"It was enough. I had changed my mind."

"That why you got those decorations?"

"A hint that I should reconsider."

"Not exactly subtle."

"Effective, though, in a way. It showed me that I can't fight them alone."

"I thought you were the man who ended range wars single handed." Their eyes met and Adams saw the challenge there. He knew what the rancher was referring to. Only a year before he had fought in a range war that had ended in a gun fight in the streets of town.

He said, "That's the kind of thing only a fool doesn't try to avoid, because it gives the kind of reputation only a fool would want—if he lives. I couldn't avoid it then, but I'm not going to do it again if I can help it. Especially for a piece of land I can't use."

"It's a good little spread."

"Yes, but I'm no rancher. Even if I could hold it, I couldn't make it pay. Yet I can sell it for what it's worth, my nuisance value is that high. You can't. You're going to be pushed off your place in the next month as surely as the sun is coming up tomorrow." He saw the shock of his words and thought, "I hope that's blunt enough for him."

"What makes you so damn sure?"

"It's my business," Frank said softly. "Mark didn't hire all those hands to play checkers. Sure he planned to use them against Oncina and the Hazels, but you were always the number one target, you can be sure of that."

"He'll find me a tougher nut to crack than them." The rancher's jaw set itself stubbornly.

Adams didn't agree, but he said only, "Maybe so, but it doesn't make much difference to the nut after it's cracked, how hard its shell was. What are you going to stop him with?"

"I've got seven good men, loyal as they come and..."

"Gunhands?"

"Of course not." Martinson sounded indignant. "One of them was a budding John Hardin before he came with me, though, and can still handle a pistol better'n most. Sarge served three hitches in the army and was the best shot in his company. And I'm no slouch myself," he added without false modesty.

Frank summed it up in one sentence. "So you have three men who can shoot and five who can't to stop twenty or thirty men, at least a dozen of them professionals."

"I know." The older man's voice was sharp, bitter. "What am I supposed to do, go out and shoot myself to save them the trouble? Just what are you getting at, anyway?"

He had stirred the rancher to the point of admitting his worry. There was nothing left but state his proposition and hope the other was troubled enough to consider it. "I'd appreciate your hearing me out before you make any decisions."

Martinson cut him off with a gesture. "I'm listening."

Frank picked up a spoon and began turning it between his fingers. He caught his reflection in its bowl, grossly distorted with pointed head, bulging eyes, bulbous nose and practically no chin. One part of him laughed at the image, while the other searched for the right words. At last he said, "Even now the Chain Link should be worth four thousand dollars; if it could be held. It's not worth a penny to me, though, except to sell. Your Lazy M is worth four or five times that, except that you can't sell it and you can't hold it. I wasn't joking when I said you were going to be pushed out within weeks unless you did something damn fast."

"Such as?"

"You can't hire some extra hands?"

"Gunmen? No."

"Principle?" A little unintended sarcasm crept into Adams' voice, but the other ignored it.

"Partly. Mainly I can't afford it. Oh, I could put on a man or two at regular wages, but even if I wanted to, I couldn't pay wages to a lot of men to sit around keeping their guns oiled." The rancher's tone sharpened as he added, "What's your proposition?"

"Simply this. To throw the two places together as one. I'll put up another thousand cash which will pay for whatever hands you want to take on. And I'll help hold the place—without shooting if possible. My part of the deal will be twenty-five percent of the whole; as a permanent partnership. If we can't hold it, you've lost nothing, and you certainly have a better chance to hold it with three or four more men. It could decide Colter to drop the whole thing."

There was nothing more to say. Frank sat back and sipped his coffee and waited. There was a silence as Martinson buttered a piece of bread and bit into it. Around them the clattering of dishes and the hum of dinner conversation filled the pause. Finally Martinson said, "It's an interesting proposition."

Adams felt an abrupt letdown. The other's tone told him the answer was a rejection. He had not expected immediate acceptance, but had hoped for the questions and arguments that would mean interest. Even the, "I'll need some time to think it over," didn't help. It was a gesture of courtesy.

Frank wanted to say, "You don't have time." He wanted to shout it at the man. It would do no good. If the other changed his mind, it would not be because of any further argument on his part.

Chapter 12

For two more days Adams stayed around town, doing little except talk to the few townspeople who would talk freely, and eavesdropping shamelessly on those who would not. The general consensus seemed to be that Colter would do nothing drastic until after his case came up in court. This represented Martinson's thinking, explaining why he could believe he had plenty of time. The suit was more clever than it appeared on the surface. Frank wondered how the same people who believed Mark was responsible for Pierce's death could believe he would wait, particularly after the burning of the Chain Link.

Thursday afternoon Hippo Krale rode into Benton's Ford. Colter had been a good prophet; Martinson reacting as expected, and Hippo played his part to perfection. In spite of his odd build, Hippo was a tough man and had taken quite a beating for the promised bonus. Still playing his part, he affected a haggard expression and a stiff legged limp and told his highly colored story with a reasonable facsimile of outraged innocence.

For all his able histrionics, however, he had to play second fiddle to one of his two companions; an honor the man would have been glad to forego—he was dead. If Hippo's efforts to drum up sympathy for the dead boy were less than successful, it was because the town knew the boy as an insufferably arrogant, particularly vicious youth, who might have been hanged for rustling two years before except for his age. Nevertheless, the whole affair had the desired effect, with town generally agreeing that the Lazy M was asking for trouble it might have avoided. The more honest, but less imaginative efforts of the Lazy M rider, who had followed Hippo in, had little effect.

Krale and his companions stayed in town until dark, spreading their propaganda. Adams was just turning into the restaurant for coffee when he saw them ride for home. A minute later the Lazy M hand followed suit. Evidently Martinson had thought Hippo might go home before coming to town and he wanted to be warned if Colter should come boiling out of the J.C. loaded for bear. Perhaps he even hoped for it as representing his best chance. It was still a bad play.

Now it would be almost midnight before Hippo could reach the J.C.. Too late to do anything tonight. By the time the men were routed out, horses roped and saddled and guns checked, the moon would be down and, with it, the light they needed to navigate the rough terrain between the two places. They would be too afraid of an ambush to use the road.

Adams stepped into the restaurant and found a place at the marble topped counter where he sat pondering Martinson's action. It had been foolish, certainly, because it hastened trouble he was not ready for. Perhaps he thought that by showing he wouldn't be pushed around, he could scare Mark off. More likely he was just determined to meet every thrust head on and either beat it back or go under fighting. It sounded like him; a stubborn, prideful

87

man with more courage than sense. He had taken Colter's bait, and it wouldn't be long before the trap closed. Whether he would accept the help he needed before it did, Frank couldn't guess. Probably not. He hoped the Lazy M owner had at least taken his suggestions about defending the place.

He had seen the ranch house only once, but he had viewed it with a professional eye. He had not been able to resist throwing his observations at the rancher when the latter, boasting about the strength of the place, had said, "That place is built like a fort. I could hold it till doomsday if I had to."

"Doomsday must be damn close," Frank answered. "I could take a third of the J.C. crew and knock you out in an hour—and not lose a man doing it." He felt a grim amusement at the other's look of shocked disbelief and injured pride. "I'm not boasting. I know that sort of thing in my business. How are you planning to cover the west side, the side toward the barn?"

"From the windows on that side, of course. How else?" The rancher's tone suggested that the question was slightly ridiculous. "The logs under those windows are fourteen inches thick and the sills are ten inches of solid oak. You couldn't ask for better cover'n that. Specially if we throw a couple of sand bags up on the sills." This was a last minute thought, tossed in to strengthen his position.

"Fine," Frank said, "but anybody who's going to shoot from there has to be alive to do it. There's nothing between those windows and the ones on the other side; no partitions, no fire place—nothing. From those east windows the ground slopes to the edge of the woods. Just right for someone shooting through them to be dropping lead right under the ones on the other side. Put three or four rifles up there and a mouse couldn't live two minute along the west windows."

Martinson paled noticeably as the picture became clear, belying the casual way he said, "Oh, we can block off those windows easy enough. A couple of..."

"Sure, it's simple." Frank's voice was caustic. "Now that you know about it. Your best bet is to cut some loopholes up near the roof. The point is, you didn't know about it."

Martinson was an honest man. "You're right," he said. Then, after a moment's hesitation, "What else?"

"The shed against the back wall." With the handle of a fork, he pressed an L shaped diagram into the tablecloth, and added a small square to the foot of the L. "There's your shed. You've got two windows covering the front of it, but at an angle so that there's about five yards right in front that are out of sight. Your outhouse is only a couple of yards further. It would be easy for someone to reach the outhouse unseen, and two running steps would take him across the open space. What chance would you have to stop him in that length of time? None, if he broke quickly,. Chances are, all he'd have to bring to cook your goose literally would be his own matches, because I'll give ten to one you keep your coal oil back there."

Martinson grimaced wryly. "He wouldn't even have to bring them. There's an extra box back there, too." Carefully he pressed out a wrinkle in the red checked tablecloth with short, thick fingers, frowning as it rose up again on each side of them. Finally he smoothed the entire cloth with a sharp tug that rattled the dishes. "We'll have to cut loopholes through the kitchen wall, too."

"That'll help, but remember that I saw those things in ten minutes. God knows how many Colter has marked. Another thing, if he doesn't see the place as a trap instead of a fort, he'll hit you somewhere else. You still have a ranch to run."

Well, maybe now Martinson would decide he needed help, even though it was quite clear that he wasn't overly fond of the only likely source of help; one Frank Adams. He would have to decide soon. Mark would want to hit while it was still a retaliatory move, and he would want to make it quick and decisive.

Frank dropped a spoonful of sugar into his second cup of coffee, stirred it and lifted it to his lips. Then he set it down untasted. A sudden chill rode along his spine. Down the counter a new arrival was being congratulated on his acceptance by one of the town's young ladies. The details of the conversation escaped Adams. Only the last two words registered.

"When," one of the others asked.

"Tonight," the young man answered.

Coming when his mind was concerned with time, the words had the impact of a blow. Frank knew instantly that it was the answer. It explained why Hippo brought the dead man directly into town instead of going to the J.C. first. It explained why the third rider stayed with him instead of taking a report to Colter and why Hippo had repeated so often his threat of what Colter would do, "When he heard about it." Lastly it explained why Hippo had stayed in town so long. The propaganda purpose had been served in the first hour.

Now there was a Lazy M rider on his way home to report that the J.C. was just hearing about the incident. He would be wrong. Colter already knew about it, had arranged to know about it as it happened. How he was moving in for the kill. Why should he wait? He had his excuse and he knew the Lazy M's weaknesses. If he waited, something might change. Adams left the restaurant with his coffee untouched.

As he swung into the saddle, he knew he would be at least an hour behind the Lazy M rider. He hoped the J.C. would delay its attack that long, but half a mile from the Lazy M he heard the first burst of gunfire and, a moment later, saw the glow of a firelit sky. His first thought was that the house had been touched off, but as he topped the last ridge, he saw that it was a haystack near the corral, burning furiously and sending a fountain of sparks straight up into the quiet night air.

Reining in at the top of the ridge, Adams reached into his saddlebags for a pair of field glasses. For several seconds he swept the lighted area with the glasses, trying to judge what had already happened and anticipate what would come next. There was grim evidence that the defenders had been sufficiently lulled by the false report for some of them to bed down in the bunkhouse. It was a long run from the bunkhouse to the main house. A half clothed body, stretched on the ground between the two, told its own story.

Surprise hadn't been entirely one sided. Occasionally, flashes near the eaves of the house told Adams that his advice about loopholes had been followed. Another body lying in the dust in front of the barn showed that the attackers hadn't discovered this until they had confidently started to move in on that side.

There were about fifteen in the attacking force. Probably all the gunhands on Colter's payroll. This was what they were being paid for. Whoever was leading them seemed to have seen the same weaknesses he had seen. A sudden sense of confidence began to replace the uncertainty and lack of sure purpose that had plagued him since coming to Benton's Ford.

The Lazy M lay in a shallow depression between two lightly wooded ridges. Behind it was a gradually widening stretch of rolling rangeland, completely without shelter. The J.C. would have come this way, where the moist earth would muffle the sound of their horses. They would have left their mounts at the edge of the wood and moved on foot along the ridges to form a rough three-quarter circle around the buildings, one side pressed in to include the barn. There was no reason to cover the open area they had come in on. To anyone on foot, it would be a death trap.

Yet this was the way they would have to go—if they went at all. He would need horses and by the look of things, he didn't have much time. It would have to be the J.C. mounts then. Those on the east side would require too much luck to find in this light. On the other side, however, just over the ridge and paralleling it, was a narrow path which he had ridden along the day he had examined the place. Although badly overgrown with weeds, it was free of brush, and offered two or three good places to leave horses where they could be gotten quickly. Mentally he crossed his fingers and prayed that he had guessed right about how they had arrived.

He dismounted when he reached the path and led his horse slowly. The low hanging moon gave barely enough light for him to find his way. Small trees and bushes crowded close on either side, making a wall of blackness broken occasionally by a shapeless patch of gray where a grassy vale poked finger-like from the path. He had passed three of these and, nearing the open graze, was beginning to wonder if he had guessed wrong. Then, to his right and slightly behind him, he heard a horse snort and paw at the ground.

Pulling his own mount's head down, he looped the reins around a protruding root and moved stealthily toward the sound. His feet made soft whispering sounds in the dew-moist grass, seeming to shout of his approach. The faint light played tricks on his straining eyes, bringing every shadow to ghostly life; animating every tree and bush until a dozen enemies seemed to be moving in on him. Drops of sweat rolled down his sides under his shirt, making the shirt cling to his back.

He had gone some thirty yards when the shadows took on an undeniably animal form, and in a moment he was among the horses. Still there was no sign of the guard. He wondered if his approach had been heard and pictured the guard crouched down in some shadow, waiting for a chance to slip a knife between his ribs. The thought sent a chill down his spine.

He forced his fingers to ease their grip on his gun butt, and began to probe the shadows for some sign of the man. Luck helped him. A few feet up the slope, he saw a pinpoint of light swing in a short arc. It puzzled him at first, then he recognized it. His man was carrying a dark lantern. Now that he thought of it, he realized that the already lighted but covered lantern was the only feasible way to mark the location of the horses if they were needed quickly.

Evidently the lantern cover didn't fit perfectly and a speck of light flickered as the lantern swung in the guard's hand. Crouching low, one hand feeling the ground in front of him, Frank inched toward the man, circling slightly in order to outline him against the faint glow of the dying fire. A dozen feet from him he straightened and eased around the trunk of a gnarled oak. He was leaning forward for the last few steps, when the guard, conscious of some alien sound, spun around and looked directly at him. It seemed impossible that he could miss seeing the figure by the tree. Adams froze there, waiting expecting any second to have the lantern flash on and bathe him in light. He found himself squinting against the expected glare, and his thumb sought the hammer of his gun.

Then one of the horses stamped nervously and the guard swung quickly that way then, recognizing the sound, relaxed and turned back to the scene below. Frank lifted his gun, leaped forward and brought it down solidly against the side of the other's head. The man fell like a log.

From here he had a fair view of the Lazy M. The firing had dropped off to a few scattered shots, and he was wondering how to locate the attackers at this end, when there was a sharp burst of firing all along the line. At its height, two figures leaped from the shadows behind the outhouse and raced for the shelter of the shed at the rear of the house. Again it was exactly as Frank had visualized it. He had the odd feeling that his mind was being read; that someone was sitting back with a crystal ball plagiarizing his very thoughts.

As the men sped across the open ground, Adams watched and wondered. His answer came when they were well within the area of supposed safety. There was a flash from the depths of the shed and one of the figures stopped short as though he had run into an invisible wall, took a hesitant backward step, and collapsed into a motionless heap. The other man, however, lunged head first in a long, rolling dive that took him into the shelter of the woodpile as the next shot passed harmlessly over his head.

They should have used a shotgun, he thought angrily. If the man could go on to complete his mission, Frank would have to work fast. Even given the kind of luck he had had with the guard, he couldn't hope to eliminate any appreciable number of the attackers. The horses were the only answer, which meant running a veritable gauntlet of rifle fire unless he could eliminate at least the last man at this end.

He moved down the slope toward the man. He stayed erect. The light was that subtle degree better so that he would no longer blend with the shadows. Yet he could not be recognized and might well be mistaken for the guard. He spotted his target and had eased to within a few feet when a sudden shout almost startled him into betraying himself. There was a note of triumph in the sound. The reason was clear. The shed was on fire; a fire that spread so rapidly he knew they had used kerosene. "I wonder if they brought their own," he murmured and laughed without humor.

This was his best chance. He stepped forward boldly, dropped to one knee and, for the second time in as many minutes, knocked a man senseless with the barrel of his gun. He had been sure the darkness and noise would conceal his presence from the next man, a full ten yards away, but this one must have had the eyes or ears of a nocturnal animal. He gave a startled yell and swung around, rifle blazing. Frank threw himself to the ground, imagining he could feel the wind of the bullet against his cheek. The man was only a shapeless shadow against the firelight. Lying on his side, he triggered three shots at it. The shadow reared up, staggered a few steps and fell with a groan.

From further along the line someone called, "You hit, Al?"

Some sort of answer was necessary. Adams tried a short, toneless, "Nah."

Whether it worked, or whether the silence that followed showed suspicion, he couldn't guess, and he had no time to find out. As quickly as possible he returned to the horses, picking up the guard's rifle and lantern on the way. A quick flash of the lantern showed five horses. It would have to be enough, time was running out for the men in the house. It still took close to five minutes to lead the horses down the path and out into the meadow. There was no cover here except the darkness. For most of the way that might be enough if they had been staring into the growing fire as he hoped.

Apparently he guessed right. He was well within the circle of light when an excited voice called out, "What's them horses doin' out thar?"

"Somebody's takin' them in," another answered. "Cut him down, damn it! Cut him down!"

Adams leaned along the neck of his mount and urged the horses into a full run. The outhouse loomed up in front of him. He swung to the left, to accept its momentary shelter, when a man suddenly stepped from behind it, a pistol gleaming in his rising right hand. Frank swore. He had forgotten this man, who had to be somewhere. It was the kind of mistake that could be fatal. He had only one chance. Slashing his mount hard, he drove it straight at the figure. He still expected to feel the shock of the bullet and was surprised when the other hesitated.

This man had been staring into the flames, too, and it took him an instant to locate his target. He fired hurriedly before leaping desperately aside—and missed with both tries. His shot was too wide, his leap not wide enough. He avoided Frank's mount, but not the next one. A welling scream was cut off, before it could be voiced, by a solid thud, and the man was hurled a dozen feet through the air.

Adams called out as he raced into the yard, both to identify himself and to get the Lazy M ready to mount quickly. It wasn't necessary. There was only one possible reason for these horses being brought in. It was an unexpected gift that no one was inclined to question. Two men were already outside when Adams pulled up into the comparative shelter of the inside corner of the house. Another was straddling the window sill, helping a wounded man out.

They were moving targets as they spurred through the widening circle of light toward the dark of the meadow. Still one of the horses was hit hard and began to buck. Its rider clung grimly to his seat until another pulled up beside him and dragged him clear. The horse ran on a few yards, then its front legs buckled and it spun into an almost graceful somersault.

A rider swore sharply and clamped his hand to his shoulder, but shook his head as Adams started to swerve toward him. Then they were out of it with only the danger of possible pursuit. With two horses now carrying double, this was a real danger; one which materialized almost immediately. They had angled away from the expected pursuit and had gone about a quarter of a mile when the J.C. reached the meadow. Frank spurred to the front shouting to the lead riders to swing to the right. The move was resisted at first, it was obvious they would lose ground, but he kept a steady pressure until they complied. Their lead had been cut to two hundred yards by the time they had completed a wide half-circle.

Taking a rifle from one of the doubled riders, Frank dropped back to wait. One of the others, understanding his play, dropped back with him. Together they waited in the anonymity of the darkness as the J.C. riders edged into the line between them and the fire.

Then the pursuers were cardboard cutouts silhouetted against the light. In unspoken accord the two men raised their rifles and laid a murderous fire into the group. On the first shot a horse went down, catapulting its rider over its head, and a moment later a rider, hit hard, slumped forward in his saddle while his mount came to a nervous halt. The rest angled sharply to the left, but by riding straight across with them Frank and his companion kept them pinned against the firelight while keeping up their steady fire.

It was too much for the J.C. riders. A few turned and spurred madly away. The rest dropped to the ground and began probing the darkness with return fire.

"Time to be moving," Frank called urgently and spun his horse.

"Reckon so," the other answered.

Crouching low in the saddle, they spurred after the rest of the Lazy M. There was no further pursuit.

Chapter 13

The hoofbeats of the fast ridden horse, which had awakened Ann Holman, were fading into town and she was drifting back to sleep when the sound of more horses on the road stirred her again. She sat up, hugging her knees, and looked out the window. In the pale light, she could just make out a shadowy pair of horsemen moving at a walk along the road fifty feet from her window. A moment later a wagon came into sight, another rider beside it. Further back were two more.

The man beside the wagon leaned over and Ann could hear his voice clearly as he said, "Hang on Dave, we're most there."

The vague figure on the wagonbed said, "I'm all right." Ann recognized the voice as Dave

Martinson's. The pain in it belied the statement, giving her a hint of the seriousness of the situation.

She swung her feet to the floor and reached for her robe, then hesitated. The first horseman had undoubtedly gone ahead to alert the doctor. While she had gradually taken over from her sister as Dan's unofficial nurse, her experience was very limited and she wondered if she would be any help in something serious. Still she knew and liked Dave, and with Margaret out of town... hesitancy ended with these thoughts and she began dressing.

There was a light knock on her door and it was pushed open far enough for her mother to look in and ask, "Is there something wrong, dear?"

Ann described what she had seen. "I thought perhaps I could help."

"Of course. Your father is awake. He will drive you in."

"No thank you, Mother. I can be there before Dad can get Duke hitched."

Her father's voice came from the other room. "I'll walk in with you, anyway." A second later he appeared, stocking footed, tucking his shirt tails into his pants.

A group of horses in front of the Palace Hotel showed that the first floor room, which occasionally served as an emergency hospital, was in use. They entered the lobby and saw a half dozen bone weary Lazy M hands slumped in the chairs around the room. At the desk the foreman, Hartong, talked quietly with the night marshal, while nearby, Ann noted with surprise, stood Frank Adams. It was he who understood her presence first and, taking her coat, escorted her to Dave's room.

The Judge turned to Hartong. "Is it serious?"

"Don't think so," the foreman said. "A bullet in the thigh. Didn't break the bone. Doc says, barring complications, he should be okay."

It was an accurate prognosis. Martinson was a tough and resilient man. There was a mild fever, followed by a heavy, though sometimes restless sleep. He was clear headed when he awoke and hungry enough to eat some of the broth Ann had ready. Later Prentis returned to relieve her. After fifteen minutes of prodding, punching and pulse counting he said, "Looks like you're a lucky man, Dave."

"Oh sure! I just need a week in bed right now."

"Two," Prentis corrected blandly, "and I still think you're lucky. Half an inch either way and it might have been three times as long. Unless, of course, it had hit an artery and you bled to death before they got you here."

"I guess you're right. I shouldn't complain, anyway. I'm lucky to be here instead of burned to a crisp out at the ranch."

"That's a fact," Prentis said with unusual positiveness. "You can thank Adams for that. Why did he do it?" When Dave shook his head, the Doctor continued, "I thought I understood his buying the Chain Link and then making that play in the Staghorn, but cutting himself in on a fight he isn't getting paid for; that's going a little far. Unless he is getting paid?" Prentis looked at the rancher quizzically.

"Hell no! I can't afford his kind of money."

"Didn't think so."

"Or could I?" Martinson stared thoughtfully at the ceiling. "You know he made me a proposition?" He went on to tell the other about his talk with Adams.

"Well I'll be an Apache medicine man," Prentis said. "What next?" Then recalling the rancher's first question, "You're not thinking of doing it?"

"Why not?" Martinson asked challengingly.

"Well after all, Dave, you know his reputation; a professional gunman. Maybe a little more presentable, a little better educated than most, that's all. How do you know what he'll do once he gets a hold on the Lazy M?"

"I don't. But I've got three good reasons for not caring too much. First; if it hadn't been for him I wouldn't be here to worry about the place. Second; if I don't do something pretty damn quick I sure as hell won't have any place left to worry about. I've got a good crew, mind you, but none of them are good enough to handle what we're up against. Last; I think I can trust him. At least I don't think he's out to cheat me. I admit he's not the first man I'd choose for a partner, but just now I don't have much choice."

"I hope it's the right choice," Prentis said.

"So do I. Everything I've got is riding on it. That is, if he'll still do it. It could be a good deal for him if he can hold the place."

"Have you considered how your friends will feel about it? Whether they'll approve?" His own disapproval colored Prentis' words. It went unnoticed as Martinson said caustically, "That's too damn bad. I didn't see many of them doing anything about it. Except Jim and he might be alive today if a few more had taken the same stand. No, the ones that count will understand, and I'm not worrying about the rest. If I'd been killed last night, they'd of heaped a lot of flowers on my grave, but they'd still play poker with Mark on Saturday night and drink with him at the bar just like nothing had happened. And a year from now if somebody asked about me they'd say, 'Him? Why he got himself killed trying to steal some of Mr. Colter's land.'"

The vehemence of his tirade left Martinson breathless. Prentis swore at himself for allowing his patient to tire himself that way. With a deliberate gruffness he said, "I've wasted too much of my time on you, Dave, I've got other things to do." He dug into his bag and brought out a small, brown bottle which he held to the light. He tipped it back and forth a few times and nodded to himself. "I'll let Ann give you this, but I want you to take it, hear?"

Martinson nodded wearily. "Do something for me, Doc?"

"What's that?"

"Send Adams over to see me."

"Later, after you've gotten some rest."

"I'll rest better if I can get this settled."

The Doctor hesitated, but recognized the truth of the argument. He held up the brown bottle. "Will you take this without any fuss?"

"Blackmailer," the rancher said.

"All's fair in love and medicine."

Adams was dozing in his room when Prentis knocked on the door to deliver the message. He started right down. Then, conscious of the possibility that Ann might be there, he went back, washed up and put on a fresh shirt and tie. He needed a shave, but decided against taking the time. After all, she might not even be there.

It was her voice, however, which called, "Come in," in answer to his knock. She was pouring a water chaser to a medical dose that Martinson obviously found highly unpleasant. She answered his formal greeting with a radiant smile, the rancher, his face screwed up into a mask of distaste, managed only a disgusted "Argh," in answer to Adams', "How do you feel?" He sat up and drank the water while Ann dropped another pillow behind him. With a grimace of pain, he hitched himself back until he was sitting nearly upright, then asked for another drink. He was ill at ease, Frank realized, but he could think of nothing to say that would help.

Ann said, "Dave had been telling me about what you did for him, Mr. Adams. It was a fine thing, and we are all very grateful, even," she made a face at Martinson, "if he won't be able to say so."

"Oh, I'll say so, all right." He looked up at Adams. "You pulled us out of a spot last night." He paused, groping for words. Not finding them he said simply, "Thanks."

Ann made another face at him and he said, "That's enough, woman. Men don't go all gushy like you women. He knows what I mean." He looked at Adams for confirmation.

"That's right," Frank said and smiled. Ann was

struck by the change the smile made. He should smile more often, she thought, he's quite handsome when he does.

Martinson, however, was more interested in the business at hand. "You made me a proposition the other day. Any chance you'd still be interested?"

"Why not?"

"Things have changed. I'm not such a fool I can't see that. We're in a fight, now, which we might have avoided if I'd given your proposition enough thought. The buildings are gone, too. Of course we can make some adjustment in your percentage to cover that, if you're still interested."

Adams brushed the suggestion aside. "I told you I didn't know what I was after, but I know it's not money. Maybe I just want to start fighting for something of my own instead of money. I don't know. Whatever it is, the same deal is just as likely to get it for me. Anyway," he confessed with a fleeting smile, "I expected to lose the buildings."

The rancher looked up, caught the smile and said, "Maybe it's best it happened this way then, 'cause I sure wouldn't of agreed to any proposition that figured that way." He sank back against the pillows, tired now, but determined to finish this. "I've got a good crew, mind you," he said, unconsciously using the same words he had used earlier, "but none of them can handle anything like this. You'll have to take complete charge. I'll be sitting it out for quite a while."

"Will the crew ride for me?"

"Yes." It was spoken with absolute conviction. "If you'll have the desk clerk send somebody for them..." his voice trailed off as he grimaced and tried to shift to a more comfortable position.

Frank said, "All right," turned toward the door, then turned back again and added, "One more thing. I can take charge, but I can't take the responsibility. That's yours, like it or not. People will only see me as a hired hand. A range war isn't a pretty thing, especially the kind we'll have to fight. Are you ready to be blamed for whatever we do while you're flat on your back?"

"You're damn tootin' I am!" Martinson gave the words a biting emphasis, pain and exhaustion momentarily forgotten.

Adams nodded. "Just so you understand."

Ann was still there when he returned and Martinson had fallen into a half doze, merely grunting when he said, "They'll be here soon." It gave him a few minutes to talk with her, though it seemed like seconds, before the crew trouped in to form an uncomfortable semicircle around the foot of the bed.

Ed Hartong, the foreman, was in the center. He was the counterpart of his employer; the same square jawed, heavy browed, solid look, which seemed to indicate stubborn honesty and quiet efficiency, while not promising imagination.

Beside him was the kid, Howie Bent, whom Martinson had spoken of as a budding John Hardin. Even now, serious, attentive and a little ill at ease, there was a suggestion of strut in the way he stood. Looking at the round, boyish face, it was easy to imagine it carrying the brash insolence and overweening self assurance that were the trademarks of the Hardins and Bonneys. Actually he had never really had that kind of temperament. A sense of humor and the ability to laugh at himself had saved him. Now, although he still carried his Colt thonged down, and still practiced his draw, his dreams of gun glory were fading along with his adolescence.

Next to him was the Negro cook, Will. He was the only one who had managed a whole hearted, unselfconscious grin as he entered. His generous mouth flashed teeth, brilliantly white against the dark face, in a wide, warm smile which included Frank as well as Ann and Martinson. There was dignity in his carriage and in the face with its wide forehead and unusually high arched nose, and the eyes shone with intelligence as well as good humor. His right hand rested lightly on the bed post, surrounding the five

104

inch knob atop it as though it were a small lemon. Its tremendous size and strength was explained by the bent and withered left arm, hanging in semi-uselessness at his side.

The left arm was the only point of similarity between him and the man next to him. Injured during the escape, this man's arm was bound in a sling. Otherwise they were night and day. Where the cook would stand out impressively in any company, this man was so average, so colorless that even the most observant person would not recall him five minutes after having seen him. This was George Nieman.

The other two were Sarge and Johnny. Neither really owned those names. Sarge might have made a good sergeant; tall and erect, with the look of unshakeable steadiness about him, but he had not gotten beyond corporal in his army stint. Another legacy from this period was a jagged scar, from an Indian lance, running from his left cheekbone to his lower lip and only partly hidden by the luxuriant mustache. The latter's sandy color, in contrast to the graying hair, and the severity of the bottom cut combined to give it a strong resemblance to a boot brush, a fact he was often reminded of.

Johnny's real name was Edwin Lee. He was an unreconstructed rebel who had been born too late to have been an active one and was the more violently partisan because of it. The nickname, Johnny Reb, had been a natural. Later, when he had become less outspoken and no less bitter, it had become simply, Johnny; a dark and moody man.

This was to be his crew. The crew with which he hoped to stop a land grabber with four or five times as many men, half of them gunmen. He watched them carefully as Martinson said, "You all know Adams, here?" All but Will nodded faintly.

Will's broad grin returned as he said, "Yes sir, and I was mighty glad to meet him just when I did, too." His voice was deep, resonant and without accent.

"I guess we all were," Martinson said seriously. He

was getting tired, and pain was riding him hard now. He explained the new arrangement as briefly as possible, ending with, "Adams will be in charge. I hope you'll work with him as you would with me, but you got a taste of the kind of thing you'll be up against, last night. I won't blame anyone for drawing this time."

There was a moment of silence, then Sarge said, "Hell, I got no pressin' business anywhere else."

A low voiced chorus of agreement followed. The rancher, slightly embarrassed, said, "Thanks," and leaned back against the pillow, eyes closed.

Motioning the men toward the door, Frank said, "We'll talk outside." Facing them in the lobby, he found himself more at a loss for words than usual. There was a long, uncomfortable pause while they waited, neither friendly not unfriendly, staring at him with disconcerting directness. It was Will who saw his uncertainty and helped him out. "Glad to have you with us." he said. "And speaking for myself, I was mighty glad to have you pay us a visit last night."

"Weren't we all, Will?" Sarge said. "Look at the warm reception we gave him."

It broke the tension enough for Frank to find his voice. He got right to the point. "The J.C. has one purpose in life just now—to smash the Lazy M. And smash it completely. We can't run cattle with him after our necks like that, yet there won't be any Lazy M without cattle. I don't imagine they'll stay around very long without somebody riding herd on them." He looked at Hartong for confirmation.

"Yeah, this'll be a choice setup for rustlers, all right. They'll flock in like buzzards."

"And they'll be helping the J.C. with every head they move," Adams said.

"What do we do?" Hartong asked. It was a simple question, simply put, but the way it was asked boosted Frank's already high opinion of this crew.

"There's only one way I know to beat a setup like this; turn Apache. We have to be just as tough, just as ruthless, because we have no more choice than the

Apache does. There is no other way. It means shooting from ambush, knifing in the dark. It won't be nice, and it won't be easy. We'll have to keep moving, hit and run, hit and run, and all the time we have to keep from being hit ourselves. Our first mistake may be our last. Colter can make several without being knocked out. I think he'll make them. He's made a couple already."

"Pierce?" Sarge asked.

"If he's responsible, yes. He knew it would be a mistake, that's why he wanted an outsider to be blamed."

"And the other?"

"His crew. It takes time to build a tough, working crew that might not shoot as well, but who'll fight out of loyalty, so he brought in a bunch of second rate gun hands and let them sit around oiling their guns while the regular hands pounded their asses all day for their wages. So when trouble breaks, the regulars will step back and let the guns earn their pay. It always happens. Colter should know that."

"Maybe he does an' doesn't think it matters," Hartong said. "'t still leaves him quite a passel of gun hands."

"True. But no matter what people think, they aren't paid to die. When that becomes too likely, they quit. Let just a few quit for that reason and the rest will follow. That's going to be our job; to convince them the odds on staying alive aren't good enough."

"What's to stop him from hirin' on some more as fast as they quit? Nieman asked.

Sarg said, "When the rats start desertin' the ship, you don't see any new ones troopin' aboard, do you?"

"He'll get a few at first," Adams said. "With money and time he might keep getting them. I don't think he's got that kind of money and you'd be surprised how fast credit dries up in a range war. We have to keep him in one and we can't give him any breathing room.

"Making the first ones quit is going to be a dirty job.

Damn dirty. When Dave offered anybody his time, he was thinking of the odds against us. I'm making the same offer because I know what we're going to have to do. Don't have any doubts, it won't be pretty."

He stopped there, staring at the floor, waiting for an answer. It was slower in coming than it had been with Dave, partly because they owed him no loyalty, partly because they had been given a sobering new thought. It was Sarge who spoke first. "After last night, you could tell me I had t' take scalps and my only worry would be whether my knife was sharp."

"I reckon there's nothin' like near roastin' to death to make a fella unsqueamish in a hurry," said Howie. "Anyway Tod Brown was a good man." It was the only mention made of the underwear clad figure in the ranch yard.

Adams nodded his thanks. "I have a couple of men coming in. They're not gun hands, but they know their way around in this kind of thing. They lost their own place, in Wyoming, in a deal like this. They'll be signing on as regular hands and, if we're still in business when this is over, they'll probably stay on." This wasn't entirely true. If he knew Paul Lescout and Murray Steinholder, they wouldn't be thinking only of riding wages. If the Lazy M was still in business, the chances were the J.C. wouldn't be. When a big outfit fell apart, there was always a chance that a couple of enterprising men could pick up some of the pieces.

These two were enterprising. He had first met them running guns into Mexico. At other times they had tried their hands at smuggling in the West Indies, running a faro table in a boom town, prospecting in Apache territory, operating a traveling carnival, and a dozen other short lived enterprises, not invariably more legal than profitable. They had accepted profit or loss with complete good humor. Until Wyoming. They had spent two lean years building something by hard, honest work and then a land grabber had bought off the law and run them out. They were resentful enough to welcome another fight.

When the men had left, he went up to his room and shaved. He had finished, and was wiping the lather from his face, when he paused to stare at his image in the mirror. Slowly he raised his finger and laid it along his upper lip. He took it away then put it back. There was no doubt about it, the mustache made him look older. Thoughtfully, carefully he took his razor and brought it up to his face.

Minutes later he found a seat in the restaurant from which he could see the hotel entrance, and began to nurse a cup of coffee. His patience was rewarded. Dan Prentis came down the street and turned into the hotel. Soon afterward Ann came out. By careful timing he managed to step from the door just as she passed. He put on an expression of surprise and said, "Good evening, Miss Holman."

"Good evening," she answered with a smile that somehow suggested he hadn't fooled her in the least.

He said, "If you don't think people will be too shocked, I'll see you home."

"I think they'll survive. I'm not worried, anyway."

It was a three minute walk to her house. They managed to make it fifteen.

Chapter 14

The first break in the J.C. forces came where it would have seem least likely and through no effort of theirs. Ben Dutcher sat on the edge of his bunk, back against the wall, one leg stretched along the bunk's edge, and methodically thumbed tobacco into his pipe bowl. It was his second pipeful and by the time he had it drawing to his satisfaction the air in the small room, a partitioned off end of the bunkhouse, was turning blue. The growing closeness of the room went unnoticed by Ben, plunged as he was in deep and not entirely pleasant thought.

It was the afternoon following the attack on the Lazy M. Normally he would have been busy with the routine of ranch work. He could not recall when last he had taken time off in the middle of a work day, but he wanted to be by himself for the serious thinking he grudgingly admitted he should have done long before.

He and Mark had been close friends when they had ridden for the Double O in Texas. It had been a good time in their lives. The only evidence of the driving ambition that was turning Mark into a land grabber now, was his grim struggle for the foreman's job. His hatred of smallness had only been hinted at by his refusal to join Ben in starting their own place. "I'd rather shovel manure on a big place that people respect, than live like a king on a two bit spread that nobody ever heard of."

Then accident had given him his own place. He had brought Ben with him as foreman. If Mark had been a good foreman of the Double O, Ben was a better one on the J.C.. He had worked as hard and built with as much pride as though the place belonged to him. When Mark's poker luck added to the size of the place, Ben's pride increased proportionately. He became completely chauvinistic, closing his eyes to the unfairness or injustice of anything calculated to benefit the J.C..

He was too logical a man to blind himself indefinitely to what the J.C. was becoming, or what was happening to him in the process. Looking back, he could see a definite change from tough but fair, to brutal and callous. He didn't know where it had begun, but somewhere along the line they had started to run roughshod over their smaller neighbors. He remembered beatings he had handed out to "whip them into line," like Alix Zbloy who had built a fence where Mark didn't want a fence, or Bud Parks who had claimed an unbranded calf.

Then there had been the hanging of the McNiel brothers. Thinking of it now, Ben was sure that Mark had been less concerned with the rustling he had used as an excuse than with the tiny wedge the McNiel land drove into his own back yard. There had been other things, isolated incidents, the memory of which he had pushed back into a corner of his mind where it might have remained except for recent events.

There had been the bringing in of a gun crew, the purpose clear from the first. Ben could have stepped out then. Instead he had gone along with every move, letting the end justify the means; the hiring of Adams to kill Pierce, the burning of the deserted Chain Link and the not deserted Lazy M. He had administered the beating to Adams without question, closing his mind to what was implied by Mark's suggestion to break the man's gun hand. He might have continued that same blindly loyal attitude except for a cynical reference by Hippo Krale to the kid over whose body he had shed his crocodile tears in town.

Jerry had been no good. A careless worker, a constant complainer, a confirmed goldbrick and, almost certainly, a rustler. No one had shed any genuine tears over his passing. But there was something in Hippo's voice as he said, "Well, the kin was finally of some use 'round here," that suggested Jerry's role was assigned to him rather than being a matter of chance. It was only a hint, but it raised questions in Ben's mind which, for the first time, he couldn't dismiss merely by turning his thoughts to something else.

Why had the kid been taken at all? Of all the crew he was the least likely candidate for the job; the least dependable, the most likely to boast afterward. Nor had it been chance selection, made because he happened to be around. He had been sent for. Why? The answer was hard to admit, but equally hard to doubt. The part he had played was the part he had been chosen to play. Ben remembered Mark's casual, "It would be even better if we got somebody shot, but I'm afraid I'm not paying enough to get any volunteers for that." Well, somebody had been shot, but he hadn't been a volunteer.

No, the kid hadn't been any good, but he had still been one of Ben's crew. To sacrifice him that cold bloodedly was something Ben could not accept. It made him examine the J.C. as it was now and see how much it had changed.

Suddenly the smoke filled room seemed to be stifling him. With an abrupt, angry motion he pushed himself up from the bunk, crossed to the door and flung it open. The only men in sight were a quartet of gunhands playing blackjack in the shade along the bunkhouse wall. Not wanting to join them, he turned toward the barn. Rounding the corner, he saw Red Smyth seated on a bench by the door. Red, the first man on the J.C. payroll, was one Ben had always liked. He crossed to the bench, put one foot on it, and leaned back against the wall. Looking down at an unbooted foot, which Red had propped up on an empty nail keg, he asked, "How's it coming?"

Red rotated the foot slowly, experimentally, flinching slightly at one point, and said, "Pretty good,. I should be back in the saddle in a couple of days."

"I wouldn't rush it," Ben said. He didn't really want to smoke any more, but it gave him something to do with his hands to pull out his tobacco pouch and refill his pipe. He extended the pouch to Red, who said, "Thanks," and pulled a blackened corncob from his pocket.

Ben let his gaze wonder slowly around the ranch. "You think the place has changed much since you first came, Red?"

Smyth looked up from the harness he was mending, eyebrows lifted sharply. "Why I reckon it has, some," he said.

"How?"

"Well, it's a lot bigger. More grass, more buildings, bigger crew. Yeah, I guess it's changed quite some."

"For better or worse, Red?"

The question puzzled Red, who knew Ben's pride in the place. He avoided a direct response by saying, "I

113

don't know, little of both, maybe. Most people would say better, I guess. The boss could get a lot more for it now, that's for sure."

"I'm not asking most people, Red. Would you rather be working here now, or the way it was a couple years ago?"

"Well, that's hard to say. I reckon, everything considered, I sorta go for a smaller place. One where you know everybody in the bunkhouse by the way they snore. Way it is now, is big, though. Some fellows like a big crew." Red looked up inquiringly, wondering what lay behind this line of talk.

Ben pulled quietly on his pipe and stared toward the far hills. Finally, arriving at some decision in his inner conflict, he took his pipe from his mouth and began knocking out the embers against the heel of his hand. He struck so violently that, at the second blow, the stem broke and sent the bowl spinning to the ground at Red's feet. Picking it up, Red examined the break. "Too bad, Ben, that was a good pipe."

"Even good things don't last forever," Ben said. There was a trace of bitterness in his voice. With thumb and forefinger he flipped the broken pipestem away, watching it spin end over end on an arching path toward a nearby trash barrel. "There's a place over near Brownsville, the Broken Wheel, that could use a good man. Boss is Bob Flack. If you should go over that way, tell him I sent you."

Certain that Ben wouldn't fire him this way, Red didn't know quite what to make of this suggestion. He made an elaborate project of relighting his pipe as he groped for an answer. It wasn't necessary. After a moment's pause. Ben went on, "As for me, I figure on heading down toward Arizona, maybe even out to California; see a little of the country before I tie on with another outfit."

Red froze, a lighted match poised in mid air, staring at Dutcher in frank astonishment. Only when it began to scorch his fingers did he remember the burning match. He dropped it quickly, carefully grinding it into the dirt with his boot heel. Still looking down, he asked, "You quitting?" He couldn't keep the disbelief out of his voice.

Ben was several seconds answering, as though unwilling to commit himself. At last he said, "Yeah, I guess I am."

"I'll be damned! Why, Ben?"

"Guess the place got too big for me, too, Red."

Their conversation had become jerky, interrupted by long pauses. Several seconds went by before Red said, "When?"

When Ben answered, it was with the finality of a man burning all his bridges. "Right now," he said. Without another word he turned and strode purposefully toward Colter's office.

As he approached the door a tired, dusty little man came out, nodded shortly and turned toward the bunkhouse. His presence stirred Ben's curiosity, for he had driven the supply wagon to town earlier and Ben hadn't heard it return. Automatically his glance went to the wagon shed then to the rear of the mess shack, but could find the wagon at neither place. Shrugging off his puzzlement, he pushed into the office.

Mark was there with Hippo Krale. He waved Ben to a chair as he completed some instructions to Hippo, but Ben contented himself with leaning back against the door frame. Having made his decision, there was no hesitancy on his part when, a moment later, Mark turned to him questioningly.

"I've decided to draw my time," he said with characteristic directness. "Though I figure on waiting till morning to leave if it's okay." He took a certain wry pleasure in the silence that followed.

Finally Mark grinned uncertainly, convinced that this was some kind of joke. "You kidding?" he asked. He knew the answer. Ben's sense of humor didn't run along these lines.

Ben shook his head and Mark exploded. "What the hell! What's wrong with you, anyway?"

"Nothing, Mark. Just tired of the job, that's all. Want to try my luck at something else, somewhere else."

"Kind of sudden ain't it?" Hippo sneered. "Sure you ain't lost your guts now that Adams has gone in with the Lazy M?"

Dutcher turned to stare at Hippo, without anger, but with a calculated coldness that sent a shiver up the ugly man's back.

Colter said, "Don't be a fool, Hippo. Look, Ben, if it's more money..."

Ben waved the suggestion aside. "It isn't." Still staring at Hippo, he asked, "You kill the kid?"

"And what's it to you?"

"If he did, it wasn't on my orders," Mark said quickly. "And I didn't know anything about it."

"Now that you do, do you give a damn?"

"Frankly no. Listen, Ben, the kid was no damn good. You know he was rustling our stock on the side. It was only a matter of time till we caught up with him, and it would have meant a hanging when we did."

"Maybe, but he was still one of my crew until then. A bullet in the back was no way to end it. We could of fired him if we didn't want him."

"Then we would have had him rustling full time instead of just part-time, that's all. He was just no good. Nobody is that rustles from the outfit he works for. He was due for a hanging. This way was better. Quick and sudden. He never knew what hit him. And for the first time in his life he was of some use."

"That's the important part, isn't it, that he was more good to us dead?"

"Knowing what he was, why not?"

"Maybe no reason, Mark. It doesn't matter anyway. That's not why I'm leaving. I just thought it over carefully and decided I want to move on, that's all."

It was the last sentence that told Mark he had no chance of changing Ben's mind. But he had to try. Dutcher was too good a man to lose. He argued earnestly for half and hour before finally giving up

116

with a gesture of defeat. "Well, Ben, I'll be damn sorry to see you go, you know that, and I sure wish you luck."

His sincerity stirred memories of their past friendship, tempting Ben to beg him to forget his land hunger and let things return to the way they had been. It would be no use. Ambition was a spur, driving Mark relentlessly. He could value friendship, but he could not let it stand in his way.

Ben packed next morning, amazed at the amount of useless trivia he had acquired in his few years here. Ruthlessly he discarded everything except the bare essentials, blanket roll, extra clothing, mess gear and rifle. As he was packing he heard a wagon on the road outside and, glancing out, saw another supply wagon heading for town. There was an extra guard on the seat and half a dozen riders strung out behind it.

He had heard the story of the missing wagon from its driver, Tony Checco. "I was coming back from town with a full load when this bastard Adams an' one o' the Lazy M bunch stopped me jus' this side o' the bridge. They made me strip the team an' run 'em off. Then I had t' unload every God damn thing an' dump it in the river. Everything 'cept the stove oil. I had t' pour that over the wagon an' fire it. Then I had t' hoof it all the way back." This last was plainly his biggest complaint.

This was the beginning. The start of a harassment that could drive them crazy before it ended. It was probably bait for an ambush. Evidently Mark thought so and was willing to gamble that he could hit back hard enough to end the fight here. Even if he couldn't. Ben did not believe the Lazy M could win with this kind of fighting. He was glad he would be out of it just the same.

Packing finished, he stood by the door, letting his eyes wonder around the room. Across the lye-bleached floor was the scarred and battered desk, bare now except for the brass lamp, the shallow pen tray, and the beaten copper inkwell. The mattress on the rough bunk was bare, too, showing the indelible depression hollowed into it by weight of his big body.

He lifted his gaze to the window, then swept it around the empty walls. Not quite empty at that. A small mirror hung above the wash stand, and tacked to the wall beside it were four squares of paper. They were four impressions of the ranch as seen by a wandering artist who had spent a day and night here. The firm, sure strokes and economy of detail showed, even to Dutcher's untrained eye, that a skilled hand had been at work. Two of the scenes were of outdoor work; the roping of a calf for branding and the gentling of a bronc. The third was of the mess hall at dinner time and the last was the bunkhouse, this very building, at the end of the day's work. If he were to open the connecting door, he would view the same scene—except for the figures. These had been hardly more than suggested, but each had been caught in such a characteristic pose that, with very little prodding of his memory, he could call out their names as from a written roster.

He hadn't intended to take anything else with him, nor did he have any idea what he would do with them, still he pulled a jackknife from his pocket and pried out the tacks. Without a backward glance, he stepped through the door and closed it behind him. Ten minutes later he was in the saddle leading his pack horse through the gate.

He took the back trail, not wanting to overtake the supply wagon, and reached town just after noon, tying up in front of the bank. The teller couldn't hide his surprise as Ben handed him the withdrawal slip for his entire savings. "This closes your account, Mr. Dutcher," he said, pushing the money under the iron grill. Curiosity had replaced surprise in his glance, but Dutcher only grunted as he recounted the bills.

Swinging back into the saddle, he headed for State Street where he intended to purchase some supplies before starting off. As he moved along the street, Shultz's corral came into his sight. The memory of his fight with Pierce returned; a sour, galling thing. Not because he had lost, but because of the reasons behind the fight. He had known that Pierce was marked for death, and his only emotion had been a cold curiosity as to whether Jim was as tough as his reputation.

Looking at the corral now, he saw the ugliness of the whole thing. "A bully boy. A damn bully boy, that's what I've made of myself," he said aloud. Suddenly he had an overpowering urge to put it all behind him. "The hell with it. I'll get what I need at Burnett's." He urged his mount into a canter and rode out of town.

Chapter 15

The idea of hitting the supply wagon had come suddenly when Adams had seen it loading at the general store and had been acted on immediately, although Sarge expressed disappointment at the scale of the operation. "It sure don't make up much for what they done t' us. Mark could take that kind of thing every day of the week and never feel it."

They were seated at the big table in the hotel room next to Martinson's. Frank leaned forward to snub out his cigarette in an already overflowing ashtray. "We have to make it something bigger. Colter knows this is the beginning, knows he might run into an ambush if he sends another wagon in. He could send it to Hortonville and avoid trouble. I don't think he will. I think he'll invite it, figuring those professionals of his can knock off a few of us under any conditions."

"You figure he will walk into it with his eyes open?" asked Nieman.

"Yes."

"When, tomorrow?"

"Yes."

"And we hit it?"

"If we can find a place where no matter how ready they think they are, they won't be ready enough."

"You got a place in mind?" Hartong asked.

Frank nodded. "Just beyond the first bridge. That slope opposite the lightning-struck pine."

Six pairs of eyes stared at him incredulously. Hartong obviously voiced the opinion of all when he said explosively, "Good God, man! a starved rabbit couldn't hide on that bank."

"But an Apache could."

"I don't know about that. Don't forget that rise in the road just the other side. They can look down on that bank an' count every leaf an' twig there."

"Let's hope they think that, it's our best chance to catch them off guard. They'll have gotten past one bad spot and will be looking ahead toward another. They'll be less than human if they don't relax a little at a place that looks that innocent."

"But how can we hide seven men there, not to speak of that many horses?" Hartong asked dubiously.

"There won't be seven men, only four. And there won't be any horses, they'll be left in the timber on the other side of the field. Four of us go in on foot along the edge of the field," Adams said. "We dig in near the top of the bank. We may not have to be rabbits to hide there, but we want to be rabbits getting out after we do our shooting."

"It's a long way across that field," Hartong said.

"We won't be crossing it. There'll be two men with the horses who'll start them across before the shooting. I figure you and George for that." Anticipating Hartong's protest, Frank added quickly, "It's not just horse holding, it has to be timed right. You have to wait until the last man tops that rise, see that the field is clear, and drops out of sight. Then you bring the horses across—at a walk." He laid a careful emphasis on the last words. "That's the important part. You'll have plenty of time, it won't hurt if we

121

have to run out to meet you, but if they should hear those horses running and look up that way, we're liable to be in trouble."

"That's no lie," Howie grinned.

"You'll have to stop about twenty yards short of the bank. You don't want to be sitting targets while we're mounting up. When you see the split in that lightning-blasted pine, you're as close as you can get."

The foreman nodded thoughtfully. "Okay, you sold me," he said at last.

The sun was beginning to burn off the early morning haze when the four figures skirted the edges of the field and moved into position on the slope.

They were a weird looking quartet. All wore buckskins, or brown cloth outfits, daubed with large, irregular splotches of green paint. Regular headgear had been replaced with battered brown felts, brims raggedly serrated, crowns punctured in a dozen places and the holes used to hold short, leafy sprigs of greenery. Every face was diagonally striped with greasy soot until it no longer looked even remotely human.

Boots had been smeared with dirt, brass studded cartridge belts had been left with the horses, regular belt buckles had been covered. Even the metal parts of their rifles had been dulled with lamp black, and Johnny had even made an effort to fix some greenery to his, drawing a jeering, "Better not put it down, Johnny, you may never find it again," from Howie Bent.

"I'm more afraid that if he puts it down it'll take root and he won't be able t' pull it lose in time to do any shootin'," Sarge said.

They scooped out deep hollows in the soft earth, covering the fresh dirt with leaves and branches and "planted" two or three spruce seedlings around each hollow. Then they settled themselves for what threatened to be a long, and possibly fruitless, wait.

Minutes after they had dug in, Will topped the high point in the road and turned his sharp eyes on the slope. He was instantly struck by the innocence which Adams had mentioned. He had not expected to see the four men from there, but when he had halved the distance and still had seen nothing, he was distinctly surprised. This gave way to amazement as he drew opposite the lightning-struck pine without definitely locating anyone, and he began to wonder if, for some reason, they had withdrawn. He felt a little foolish as he called out, "If you're still up there, I ain't been able to locate you. Least not for sure."

"Good," Adams answered, his voice locating him for Will. "Now circle around behind us and keep a sharp eye open."

An hour passed, then two. A third was well started when Howie said tensely, "Here they come."

They looked across to the far hillside, where the road emerged from the timber, and saw a wagon move from the shadow into the sunlight. "Hell, there's only one extra man with it," Johnny said disgustedly.

"Maybe it ain't them," Howie said.

"It is," Frank said. Three or four dots had slipped out of the woods on each side of the wagon to join it on the road. "It figures. That was one of the danger spots. They circled to get behind us if we happened to be there."

"Gosh," Howie said, "you think they'll do that here?"

"Not unless they suspect something," Adams said. "They'll want to be on the road with the wagon until they get to the next bad spot. Then they'll swing off suddenly to catch us if we're there."

'I'm kind of glad we ain't," Howie said.

"We better get settled in," Frank said. "And remember, just two shots. I'll call the first when the wagon gets to the pine. Make that one good. If you can't find a target for the second, don't look for it—just get the hell out of here."

There was a murmur of understanding, then a brittle silence. The seconds dragged by with painful

123

slowness as though time itself had suddenly grown weary. Only the four men were aware of it, though. The pair of squirrels, leaping from branch to branch in a frantic, excited game of tag, were unaware of this strange suspension of time, as were the parent thrushes, busily feeding their young. Above their head a soaring hawk, gracefully etching invisible figure eights in the sky, knew nothing of it, nor did the mother rabbit, poking her head timidly from the hole beneath a dead tree to test the air with wrinkling nose as her offspring pushed impatiently at her heels. Perhaps she sensed some of the tension that pressed like a leaden weight on the hidden men, for she remained in the doorway.

After an eternity of slowly building pressure, time started up again with the striking of a horse's hoof on stone. A second later the first riders reached the crest of the ridge and started down the grade, followed by the waggon and then a half dozen more horsemen, riding in pairs.

Their inspection of the bank ahead of them was brief and casual, but to each of the ambushers, it seemed that every eye had immediately focused on his hiding place, piercing the camouflage and laying bare the trap. It increased the tension to the breaking point.

Yet they had not been seen. The riders had looked at the slope, found it harmless and turned their attention to the more dangerous stretch ahead. The first pair of riders passed the split pine. Frank took up the slack in the trigger and began to count. At the count of five he knew, without looking, that the waggon had reached the marker. "Now!" he said sharply and squeezed the trigger.

A drum roll of shots broke the stillness. His target was a squat, dark man in a bright green shirt with big mother of pearl buttons. One of the buttons shattered, its pieces flying out in all directions like sparks from a pinwheel. The man lurched backward in the saddle then, grabbing the horn, pulled himself upright. He clung there a second, then toppled forward until he lay against his mount's neck.

Adams had already swung his sights toward the last man in line. It was a longer shot, but the man was still sitting squarely in the saddle as he reached for his rifle in the boot under his knee. Just as he squeezed off his shot, the man's horse, excited by the sudden firing, shied nervously, spoiling his aim. It was not a clean miss. As he turned to scramble up the bank, Frank saw the rider drop his half drawn Winchester and clutch his left arm.

Then Frank was throwing himself in a rolling dive over the lip of the bank. Sarge was a half second ahead, performing the same maneuver, and a second later Johnny and Howie came over the edge running upright.

"Get down, damn it," he shouted.

They hit the dirt as ungracefully as he had just as the first searching shots cut through the air above them. They scrambled to the waiting horses and spurred hard across the field. There was no pursuit.

Two miles away they pulled up to blow the horses. Here they were joined by Will. "You can take it easy, boys," he called as he rode up. "There's nobody on your trail."

"Don't see how there could be," Howie said excitedly. "We must of knocked over six of 'em at least, maybe all."

"If we knocked over all of them, who in hell was doin' all that shootin' as you come over the bank?" Sarge said. "Squirrels maybe?"

"Those boys are professional guns," Will said solemnly. "I hear they keep shooting for six hours after they're dead."

"Well," Howie conceded reluctantly, "we might of missed a couple." He looked to Adams for confirmation.

"If we put three of four out of action more or less permanently, we did all right."

"Okay, so we didn't get 'em all," Howie said. "We

sure gave 'em somethin' to think about."

As they rode on, Frank studied the others. Howie was overly ebullient now, but he wouldn't sleep much tonight. When excitement wore off and reaction set in, he would see his man falling under his gun a hundred times. Even the justification he had would not make it easy. Howie wasn't cut out to be the gunman he had dreamed of being.

Johnny's strange bitterness would be a partial buffer against remorse as it was against exhilaration.

Sarge would be least effected. He had been through this before. Still, there was a tightness about the eyes that had not been there earlier.

The others had been further from the action and had been less touched by it. Their turn would come.

"We headed back to town now?" Nieman asked.

Frank shook his head. "There's no telling how many J.C. hands may be there. After today the marshal would need thirty deputies to keep them off our necks. We're going to have to stay out of town from now on. We'll ride over and pick up our supplies and a pack horse at Burnett's."

Chapter 16

There was a grand total of six buildings at Burnett's Corners. They racked their horses in front of the largest, a low, rambling structure, half log and half unmortered field stone. The words, "Burnett's— General Merchandise," in huge and highly ornate red and gold lettering filled the body of the sign that ran almost the full length of the building. Smaller signs; Hardware, Saloon, Groceries and Dry Goods, hung over each of the three entrances.

There was no one in sight when they entered the saloon section, but an instant later a head poked around the end of a partition on the left and said, "Be right with ya'," then ducked back before they could answer.

Half a minute later the man himself stepped through the door behind the bar, tying an apron around his ample waist. He had a big, open, friendly face and a voice to match. "Yes, sir, what'll it be?"

"You're Burnett?" Frank asked.

"That's right. Charlie, that is. Lew's out back."

Only three of them had ridden in. Will to get the supplies, Johnny to select a horse. Johnny said, "Who handles the horses?"

"That's Lew. He's out at the corral now."

Johnny nodded and without a word started for the

door.

"Straight out back," Burnett said unnecessarily.

Adams looked toward the grocery section. "Anyone back there?"

"Sure. One of the girls should be there. My wife and sister-in-law run that side of the place an' me an' Lew run this. Works out pretty good." He turned and called, "Clarissa!" Frank winced as the voice nearly blew down the partition.

There was a soft, "Yes," from the other side.

Burnett said, "Store customers fer ya'," in slightly modified tones. "That's my wife," he added. There was a suggestion of pride in his voice.

Clarissa was a plump, attractive little woman, whose voice made up in endurance what it lacked in power. She talked so steadily that they had difficulty stating their needs.

Leaving Will to complete the purchases, Frank returned to the bar. He had been through this kind of trouble before, but never failed to have his fight with nerves afterward. It was the only time he preferred bourbon to beer. He took a third of the drink into his mouth, letting it roll slowly across his tongue, then stood with one elbow on the bar, head bowed and eyes closed waiting, a little grimly, for the whiskey to bring the warm, relaxing flow that would untie some of the knots.

Recognizing the symptoms, Burnett said, "Hard day?"

Frank ran a hand across his eyes, "Yes," he said. He heard a horse move up outside and decided Johnny had made his choice already, but the heavy tread on the walk was not Johnny's. Instantly alert, he flicked his eyes to the bar mirror in time to see Ben Dutcher push through the door and start across the room. Ben was three steps into the room before he saw Adams. His stride broke and his face froze in shock. There was nothing frozen about his mind. In the next fraction of a second he considered every possibility. He was too far into the room to try for the door. To try for his gun would be worse. The only choice was to play the hand as it stood. He recovered so quickly that his break in stride was only a slight hitch and Burnett, looking at him, was unaware of anything wrong.

Without changing direction, Ben walked straight to the bar five feet from Adams. It reminded Frank of his one meeting with Jim Pierce. Ben had more reason to expect trouble. In the next minute he might have to face one of the deadliest gunmen alive, yet his voice, when he answered Burnett's greeting, was level and unafraid.

Burnett asked, "What're ya' doin' up in this neck of the wods, Ben?"

"Just want a few supplies, Charlie."

"How come the J.C.'s buyin' up here? Not that I mind the business ya' understand."

"Sorry, Charlie, this isn't J.C. business. Just a few trail supplies for me."

"Goin' on a trip?"

"Pulling out. I drew my time yesterday."

Burnett's jaw dropped in astonishment. There was a brief struggle between courtesy and curiosity. Curiosity won. "How come, Ben?"

Ben hesitated, searching for words. Actually speaking more to Adams than Burnett, he said, "You work for a place for a fair time, Charlie, and it's a good outfit. You get so's you give it everything you got. You do anything for it. Then something happens and you look around and find it's not the same place it was."

"Ya' thinkin' of the other night—the Lazy M?"

"Partly. Something like that makes you do some thinking. The place has changed, Charlie. Mark has changed. Something's driving him. Guess I can't go for night riding and moonlight shooting just because he can't stop grabbing range."

"What about shooting from alleys?" Adams asked softly without looking up from his glass.

Ben stiffened. "That wasn't me," he said. "I had my trouble with Jim, but it ended that night." He relaxed slightly as Adams didn't push the accusation and

129

added, "As far as I know it wasn't anybody from the J.C.."

"Any idea who it was?"

"No." Tension caused the wrd to come out flat, belligerent. In a less blunt tone Ben added, "All I know is that none of the men left the place after you did."

A strained silence followed and Burnett, feeling it although not understanding it, cleared his throat noisely and said, "Where ya' figure on goin' from here, Ben?"

"South. Arizona, New Mexico, maybe out to the coast. I've got a little money, I think I'll look around a bit."

"Ever think of gettin' a little place of your own? Up this way, maybe. Wouldn't cost..."

He trailed off as Ben interrupted with an emphatic, "No. I've spent my whole damn life on just two outfits. I want to see a little of the country before I tie myself down again."

"Every man's got a right to name his own poison," Burnett conceded amiably. "Sorry to see you leave, though." He placed a glass in front of Ben and looked questioningly at him, but Ben's attention had returned to Adams with a faintly challenging, 'If you're going to start something, do it,' expression.

Frank's answer was to push the bourbon bottle along the bar toward him. "Luck," he said.

Ben's eyebrows arched in surprise, not entirely masking relief. He poured his drink with a steady hand, nodded to Adams and said, "Thanks," his voice carefully neutral. A minute later he was following Burnett into the hardware section.

Chapter 17

Two days later they hit the J.C. again. Slipping up to a well guarded camp, they eliminated one of the guards with a knife and ran off their horses. As Frank had warned, it wasn't pretty, but one knife in the dark would put more pressure on the J.C.'s hired guns than a dozen daylight attacks.

The following day they rode to meet Paul Lescout and Murry Steinholder. They were pleasantly surprised to find a third man as well. He had ridden for them in Wyoming and had tagged stubbornly along even though they had warned him about what they were getting into. He would join Johnny and Sarge in answering to a false, and this time inappropriate, name. He was a dark skinned, black eyed Mexican, barely five feet two, and his name was Just Kelly. Orphaned by typhoid at five, he had wandered, half starved, into the camp of a prospector named Kelly. He stayed with him until he was fifteen. All that time he was called nothing but Little Kelly. When Big Kelly died and he had to get a job, he had given his name to the foremen as Kelly.

The man had looked at him with a doubtful, but friendly grin. "No first name, son?"

"Nope. Just Kelly."

In a joking mood, the foreman said, "Okay, Just Kelly it is," and put it down that way.

Steinholder and Lescout were both tall, lean men; the taller one, Steinholder, standing six feet six inches. They had the same deep set eyes with sharply betched crows feet gathering at the corners and there was a strong sprinkling of gray bin their hair.

Frank introduced them around, then asked, "Did you bring the horses?"

"Yep," Lescout said. "Left 'em with that plow pusher, Inglass, like you said.

"Good, we'll pick them up tomorrow. Meanwhile, I'll fill you in on things while we eat."

Putting down his empty plate, Frank said, "That's the picture, the kind of fighting we've been doing and are going to have to keep right on doing. I don't claim our chances are good. There will be no hard feelings if you don't want to join in."

Without glancing up from his plate, Steinholder said, "We already joined."

Lescout nodded agreement. "You're just making us feel to home with that kind of talk. What are your plans?"

Frank drained his cup and handed it to Will for a refill. "Just to keep hitting and running, that's all. But now we have to count on being chased as we leave. That's where your horses come in. We have to have fresh ones, and fast ones, staked out for when they press up too hard."

"What happens when they stop chasing and start pushing; camp on our trail with one bunch while they throw another in front of us to run into?"

"I'm hoping we've cut them down to size before they think of it. Or before they can get it well organized, anyway."

"I wouldn't count on it."

"I'm not."

"That's good. Where do we take the first bite?"

"Hungry?" Frank asked.

The other's eyes lifted to meet his. The burning hatred in them told him the J.C. would be paying for someone else's land grab. "Yeah," he said. "I'm hungry."

"We'll show you later. If you like the looks of it, it'll be a good chance to introduce you to them."

They had their look that afternoon and took the bite the next day. Their target, a windmill which fed a small artificial lake, was only a mile from the J.C. headquarters. At a glance a windmill here, with the river so close, might seem sheer waste. Yet for nearly five miles, steep, rocky banks kept all but a handful of cattle from the water on this side, reducing the value of its thick, high grass.

A natural basin nearby needed only a low dam and windmill to become a sizable both. A work crew was repairing the dam while a guard on the windmill platform and another at the corner of the corral kept a prosaic watch. The proximity to the ranch and the presence of the work crew had given them an unwarranted sense of security. It didn't require any particular skill for Frank and Hartong to slip to within fifty yards of the two sheds behind the windmill. This final stretch was completely open. They knelt in the shelter of some low bushes and waited.

On the other side, a third of the way to the J.C., Sarge sat with his back against a pine stump and his field glasses trained on the ranch yard. An hour dragged by before he saw what he wanted; ten or twelve horses, saddled and ready, with a dozen of the J.C. gunhands nearby.

Putting the glasses away, he drew his Colt and fired two quick shots. He mounted his horse, a distinctive dapple gray, fired one more shot, and spurred toward the pond. As he came within sight to the windmill, he seemed to see, for the first time, the danger there. He pulled to a sliding stop, then reined sharply to his left, ducked low in the saddle, and spurred desperately off in this new direction.

The entire maneuver took less than a minute, but it distracted both guards and kept the work crew pinned down, too.

The guard on the windmill platform had become alert with the first shot. Now he gave a shout of recognition. Bringing his rifle to his shoulder, he swung it to follow Sarge's racing figure. He never pulled the trigger. Two bullets from below literally brushed him off the platform. To protect Sarge, both Adams and Hartong had fired at this man before turning their attention to the other, who had stepped away from the shelter of the horse shed to see what was going on.

This second man was an old campaigner, however, who had stayed alive because he had the instincts of the hunted. Without even turning toward this unexpected danger, he dropped his rifle and dived toward the shelter of the shed. Swinging to follow the somersaulting figure, Adams saw his hurried shot kick up dust in the corral beyond. He drove four shots into the shed wall a foot from the ground, more to make the man bury himself than in any hopes of hitting him.

Behind him Hartong was holding the work crew pinned down with a slow, methodical fire. The rest of the Lazy M arrived within seconds, dragging bundles of dry brush behind them. They piled the brush against the legs of the windmill and into the doorway of the one shed, Frank warned them away from the other, not wanting to force the hiding guard into a desperate move. The brush was soaked with kerosene and, in seconds, the skeleton of the mill was clothed in flame; the shed burning beyond possibility of saving.

It had taken just three minutes. They milled around for another half minute until a dozen riders broke over the crest of the knoll where Sarge had waited and spurred madly toward them. They counterfeited momentary confusion, then they, too, were spurring

134

their mounts at top speed across the range.

Within a mile they were paralleling a twenty foot cliff a hundred yards to their left. It was here that they had decided to introduce their new recruits. These three were stretched out behind the grass fringing the top of the cliff. They noted the passage of the pursued, but their attention was fastened on the pursuers, who were approaching the shallow gully being used as a marker. They picked their targets, held them in their sights, and waited, sweating and tense.

At last Lescout said sharply, "That's it!" The three rifles cracked raggedly.

Two things kept it from being a massacre; one physical, the other psychological. When they had examined this spot the previous day, the ground had still been moist from a local shower. Today, eight hours of hot sun had sucked out the moisture and left a thick layer of powdery dust. At the first volley the J.C. riders pulled to a sliding, skidding halt and dust boiled around them, thick and opaque.

Lescout swore and poured shots indiscriminately into the dust cloud. When the dust thinned, there were two still figures sprawled on the ground. A third was desperately pulling himself into the shelter of a still kicking horse, dragging a bullet smashed leg behind him.

It should have been worse, but killing does not come as easily to the average man as he expects. Two of these men were average. Only Lescout had the emotional push, a smoldering, almost fanatical hatred, to sweep aside this mental barrier. Steinholder had as much cause for hatred as his partner, yet at the last second he hesitated, spoiling his first shot. Kelly had his moment of hesitation, too, then dropped his sights to a running horse.

If it was not a massacre, it was a serious blow. Two or three more like that, where they were badly mauled without a chance to strike back, might just make the hired gunmen decide it wasn't worth it.

135

Adams was concentrating on them, convinced that they could be, had to be, cracked.

Yet it became increasingly clear through the next few days that it wasn't going to be easy. They hit three more times, once at night, again with a knife. It was the ugly kind of fighting that Colter's hired guns would have the least stomach for. Yet they were tougher than he had hoped. If any of them quit, he hadn't heard it.

The J.C., acknowledging at last that they were in a fight, became more alert and cautious. Finally, as Lescout had predicted, they gave up the headlong chase with its chance of ambush and began a steady, organized push. The Lazy M became the hunted.

The pursuit was a net, driving them back with a steady pressure. They twisted and turned and doubled back, to no avail. The net was always there and with it, the chance of running into an ambush themselves. Five days later they had been driven twenty miles back into the hills and had ridden ten times that far getting there. Yet "there" was merely a hidden place which they had passed by two days before, arrived at by feeling their way through the dark for two hours.

They virtually fell from their saddles on the raw edge of exhaustion, knowing that by the time they had taken care of their horses, they would have less than five hours before early morning light would force them into the saddle again. The J.C. must have thrown every man who could ride onto their trail, and it was a well planned, well executed operation. Better than Adams had expected the first time. He had expected to slip back to the heart of the valley at least once, to lose their trail on the well traveled roads.

They were tired, grim men who bedded down that night. They were neither less tired, nor less grim when they resaddled weary horses in the dampness of an early morning fog. They had tried everything they know to shake themselves loose and had failed. Now they were reduced to two choices. They could try to break through, probably succeeding, but at what cost no one could guess; or they could run, leaving the valley entirely. Neither was attractive.

Unless they were very lucky, they would lose a couple of men in breaking through, possibly more. If they ran it was defeat too. Once they left the valley their chances of getting back were slim. The passes would be closed behind them, and it would take weeks to circle around to the south and, rest their horses, and try to slip back unnoticed. Chances were they could't do it. If they did, they would have to start all over, without the advantage of surprise, without the fresh remounts which had saved them twice already, and against an enemy with its confidence restored.

Hartong, who knew the county sheriff, voiced another danger. "Conners'll straddle the fence as long as he don't know for sure who'll win. The minute we get shoved out of the valley, an' it looks like Mark's got things sewed up, it'll be different. If we did get back in, we'd likely find half of Mark's gunnies wearing deputy badges and carrying warrants." The decision was pressing them as hard as the pursuit.

Nature gave them their reprieve. It started to drizzle that morning, stopping before noon with partly clearing skies. In early afternoon it clouded over again and this time the rain really came. It came as though dumped from barrels. It whipped into their faces, driven by an erratic wind which never came from any one direction for more than a second and often seemed to come from all sides at once.

They rode all afternoon through this downpour which seemed determined to extract full payment for its largess, taking some malicious delight in finding every partially dry spot and thoroughly soaking it. The ever shifting wind threw water at them in solid waves. It lifted water from grass and bush to drive it against them horizonatlly, forcing them to drop their heads to meet it. Instantly it seized the opportunity to dump gallons of water down the back of their necks.

They found shelter in a cave, five miles from their

previous camp, where they could kindle a fire safely. Here they made an effort to dry out. Sarge took off his shirt and wrung the water from it, watching as a puddle formed on the floor. "Hell," he said. "Might as well have swum all the way here."

Howie looked up from taking off his boots, eyebrows raised. "Thought we did," he said innocently.

Hartong said, "I don't know 'bout you but, for a fact, my pony was swimming most of the way. Jus' wish he'd stayed on top 'stead of swimming through the middle."

"Just proves he's got more sense than you," Sarge said. "Suppose he had been swimmin' on top and somebody turned off the water. Where would you be? Why sittin' a thousand feet up with nothin' under you but air."

"Yeah, but I wouldn't of drowned, anyway. God! I never seen the beat of this. Look at it!" He hooked his thumb toward the cave entrance where the rain was a leaden sheet. "I rode up the trail three times, and we hit a heap of weather. Damned if I remember any like this, though."

"Oh, it's a pretty fair sprinkly," Steinholder said deprecatingly. "But have any of ya' been down t' south Texas?"

Adams said, "I ran a telegraph office down in San Angelo when I was a kid. We got a few good rains in the spring, but nothing worse than this."

"You were still pretty far north, Frank. Now I remember once down near Laredo..." It started a rash of stories, each more far fetched than the last.

Will, who had started coffee as soon as the fire was blazing, called that it was ready and they all crowded back to the fire. For an hour they soaked up its warmth while, with perfectly straight faces and solemn oaths as to their truth, they spun their gems of prevarication. All but Johnny and Lescout, who had taken the first watch, and Adams entered in.

Frank regretted that he had no experience with this

sort of thing, for here was a chance to break down some of the barrier between himself and these men. They had accepted him, with reservations, because Martinson had, and they had shown their respect for his ability. Yet he was not really one of them. Steinholder and Kelly had been accepted, as had the grim, dour Lescout. Somehow he hadn't been able to break through.

At last Howie stilled all competition with a magnificent example of this particular art. There was a long silence. "Howie," Sarge said finally, "you're a damn liar." Howie beamed at the compliment.

One by one the men turned in, leaving only Howie and Frank, who had the next guard, staring silently into the dying fire.

Presently Howie broke the silence. "Were you really a telegraph operator once?"

Adams looked up, surprised. "Sure. What's so odd about that?"

Suddenly embarrassed, Howie said quickly, "Nothin'. Just that all the key pounders I ever saw were white haired old coots with store teeth, or dried up little squirts without enough muscle to pound anything else."

This wasn't it, Adams thought bitterly. It was surprise at the mention of a past not directly connected with a gun. It had happened before. People just couldn't grant him an ordinary past even in his youth. They seemed to believe he had been born, full grown, in some murky barroom with a smoking pistol in his hand.

Throughout his turn at guard, the thought continued to plague him. Could he ever change this bigger-than-life portrait of a gunman that filled the eye and mind of everyone who heard his name? Still, thinking back, they had been more relaxed tonight than at any time before. Of course Will had been from the beginning. It was his nature, as it was Nieman's nature to be reserved.

Both Sarge and Howie had seemed to loosen up a

little. How much Adams couldn't guess. Some surely. Howie still had visions of himself as the deadly gunfighter, stalking the streets of Dodge City. Frank had had these dreams himself.

Ed Hartong was still cooly distant. He had been brought up to despise gunmen. He was a fair man, though, who believed in giving a man a chance to prove himself. Nor had Johnny changed. Black Johnny; lonely, morose, unapproachable. Thinking of him, Adams decided he was the luckier of the two. He was acutely conscious of his own loneliness, but he was lonely among strangers. Johnny was lonely among friends.

The rain dropped off next day to a misty drizzle, interspersed with short, hard showers. Ignoring the probability of another soaking, Adams rode into town, getting there just as darkness fell. It was no pleasure jaunt. Some arrangement had to be made for getting supplies, which were running low, and he wanted to hear what news Martinson might have picked up in town.

The rancher was up and getting around a little with the aid of crutches. Apparently he had set up an efficient information service; he had all the news worth knowing, including some both disturbing and encouraging.

"'Nother bunch of gunhands come in on yesterday's train," he said. "Headed for the J.C.."

"How many?"

"Eight if I got the right dope."

"Hell, that brings them back to full strength."

"Not quite. One of the ones that got hit in that affair out at the pond quit. He stopped in town and got to talking to some of the new men. He must of made it look plenty grim out there, 'cause a couple of them turned right around and pulled out with him." This, at least was encouraging. It indicted that the hoped for crack might be developing.

Martinson had also made arrangements for supplies. "Les Fliepp, he's got a little place out east of

Colter, will pick them up Saturday, like he was buying for himself. He'll take them out to his place and leave them out behind his spring house."

Adams had been careful to slip into town unnoticed. Yet one person had seen him—Ann Holman. She had just come from visiting the patient, and was standing in the shadow at the end of the veranda, struggling with a balky umbrella, when the side door opened suddenly and Adams' face was momentarily lighted as he stepped quickly into the hotel.

Taking off one of her gloves, she dropped it beside a chair on the darkest part of the porch. With her excuse established, she returned to the lobby, where she allowed an eager young desk clerk to get a lamp for a search of the veranda, while she checked the Lazy M office. Martinson's room was officially that now, even to a sign over the door, designed to show that the "Lazy M Cattle Co." was a going concern.

Entering in response to the rancher's, "Come in," she said, "I seem to have dropped one of my gl..." she broke off in well feigned surprise at seeing Adams. "Why Mister Adams, how did you get here? I left only a minute ago."

He answered her as they searched for the glove, an easy task, for the room contained only four pieces of furniture in addition to the bed; a big oak desk, two chairs and an empty but impressive safe.

They had just finished when the clerk arrived with the object of the search. He accepted Ann's thanks with a pleased smile, spoke briefly to Martinson and, without a flicker of surprise, gave Frank a quick, cooly civil nod.

Frank looked inquiringly at Martinson. "He's all right," the rancher said when the man had gone. "You came in the side door, that's all he has to know. In that case he could see General Grant and General Lee standing here in full uniform, toasting each other with champaigne, and when he got home he wouldn't even tell his mother."

141

"Sounds like Doc Prentis," Frank said with a chuckle.

"Oh no." Ann said. "Dan would tell about it, all right, but it would be somebody who 'looked like General Grant' and who 'resembled General Lee,' in what 'might have been' army uniforms, drinking what 'appeared to be champagne.'"

Frank smiled and Martinson laughed outright. "That's him," Dave said. "That's him exactly." Then, by way of apology to the good doctor, he added, "But he's a damn good doc. Knows just what he's got to do and don't waste time doing it. Like with my leg here. While he was talking 'bout what it, 'might be,' and what it, 'looked like,' and what, 'could happen,' he was cutting away, and he had that slug out and a bandage on b'fore most docs would of got their coats off."

Ann accepted the not unexpected invitation to be escorted home. Again, using the muddy street as an excuse, they took the long way. Still it was entirely too short to suit Adams. Somehow this girl set him at ease as no one else ever had.

At the door she turned toward him. He had already refused her invitation to come in. Now she said, "I will see you again, won't I?" She knew how conscious he was of his reputation and realized that if she wanted to see him again, other than by accident, she would have to take the initiative. "Will you call next time you're in town?"

"There's no telling when I'll get to town again."

"When you do, will you call?"

He hesitated, then said, "If I get in again."

She understood his hesitation. "Is there no other way to end this? Some compromise, perhaps?"

"If I knew of one that would end it, I'd take it. There's no pleasure in what we're doing, believe me."

"I know. I didn't mean to criticize."

"No, it's a fair question. It's just that there is no compromising with someone like Colter. If he compromised it would only be a way of taking the first bite, it wouldn't stop him. He wants that land and he

142

means to have it. Funny thing is, even if he gets it he won't stop. He'll want more—and more. Someone has to fight him, somewhere, sometime."

They were standing in the faint light slanting through the long plate glass of the front door. She looked up at him as though to study his face, although, like her own, it was only a pale smudge in the darkness.

"I understand," she said softly. "Please take care of yourself." There was genuine concern in her voice.

In that moment he knew how much he cared for her. He wanted to take her in his arms and tell her so. Somehow he couldn't do it and let the moment slip by with a trite, "I'll try."

Ann closed the door behind her and leaned back against it. She knew how close he had been to revealing his feelings. Half aloud, she said, "He will take a lot of encouraging."

She had thought herself alone and started violently when Glynn thrust his head through the drapes at the parlor doorway and asked, "Who will? Who was that? Was that your fella'?"

Ann was not easily flustered, but the sudden rush of questions caught her off guard, and the color rushed to her face as she answered sharply, "None of your business."

Her discomfort was an open invitation to tease. He took advantage of it to announce to the world, in high singsong tones, "Annie's got a beau, Annie's got a beau."

Her, "You be quiet!" only brought a louder repitition as he danced out of range of her threatening umbrella.

The library door opened and their father stepped out. Smothering a smile, he said, "That's enough Glynn." He looked at Ann, eyebrows lifted in a faintly quizzical expression. He rarely asked her a personal question directly, and she could have ignored his look without anything being said.

Instead she said, "Mr. Adams."

She was the shadow cross his face, indicating the disapproval he did not want to voice. "I met him at Dave's. He saw me home." When he didn't answer, his face still troubled, "I asked him to call next time he was in town."

"All right." He tried to make his voice sound sincere and could not and added, "Ann, I will welcome him to this house if you wish, but for the sake of your mother and me, I ask you to remember what he is; a hired gunman. Don't get to like him too much. You will only get hurt. Even if he wins this fight, he isn't the kind to settle down to a ranch. He will drift along until he gets killed in some other range war."

"Dave doesn't think so. Neither does Mr. Lovejoy. They both think he means to stay on the Lazy when this is over."

"John said that?" He was decidedly surprised. He had a high regard for Lovejoy's opinion. The gambler had an amazing ability to judge people.

"Both of them did," Ann said.

"Perhaps I am wrong about that. Don't forget, though, the chances are that he will never be able to try. He is up against long odds."

Chapter 18

After Adams left Ann, he went directly to the stable. He slipped in through the harness room and was saddling his horse, when someone said something to the night man, then two men entered, leading their mounts. They were J.C. riders. One of them, a man called Smith, he had seen before. The other probably answered to the name of Lefty, for his tied down gun was on his left thigh.

Frank let them reach the middle of the stable floor. "Hello boys," he said.

They caught the challenge in the voice without recognizing the man in the shadow. He took a step toward them, letting the light fall across his face.

It was Lefty who recognized him. "What d'ya' want, Adams?"

It wasn't a question, it was a warning to his companion who stiffened at the name. His adams apple bobbed sharply in his scrawny neck as he swallowed. He moistened his lips with the tip of his tongue.

Frank waited, putting the pressure on them. They would be sure he had been waiting here for them.

Lefty said again, "What d'ya' want with us?"

Frank smiled. "What do you think?" There was mockery in his voice.

Lefty's voice was tight. "We got no quarrel with you."

"Maybe I have with you."

"'Bout what? I ain't never met you afore in my life."

"Oh, it's not personal. Not at all. It's just been six days since we took a cut at you boys. I decided it was time we did. You two were elected."

He was watching Lefty. Seeing that, the other man inched his hand toward his gun. Adams said, "Any time, friend. Any time." The man's hand jerked away quickly. His tongue darted out like a snake's, touching lips that wouldn't stay moist.

Lefty was the dangerous one. Frank continued to watch him, smiling a confident, derisive smile, until he was sure Lefty had steeled himself to make his play, then eased the strain by saying, "What's the matter, boys? Isn't this what you're being paid for? Or did Colter tell you there wouldn't be any danger? Only an old man and half a dozen cowhands? A push over?"

He saw the scrawny man's head jerk in a nervous nod. "Well, he was wrong. He doesn't know how wrong yet. You've only seen a sample of the kind of fight you're in. Do you know who was up on that ledge when you boys were chasing us from the pond?" He expected no answer. Lefty held himself stiffly alert, careful to make no sudden moves. The other continued to touch his lips with a nervously darting tongue.

"Pappy Yates and Joel Crawford," he answered for them. He could have mentioned tougher fighting men, though not many, and none who used a knife like Yates. "And where Pappy goes, Billy Joe and Clarence aren't far behind. I figure they'll be here by the end of the week. They'll probably bring Charlie Kirkshaw with them, too."

Frank could see his lie having the desired effect on Smith. He wondered how the man had managed to pass himself off as a gunman. Lefty was less easily read. "Then Mark's going to find out how rough

146

things can get. Come to think of it, maybe I'll let you tell him. The boys out there might like to know what they'll be facing."

Plainly Smith thought it a very good idea and was prepared to act on it immediately. With a jerky, eager nod, he quickly began to edge toward his horse. Adams said, "Hold it. Better drop those guns first. I wouldn't want you to get any ideas after you leave."

Lefty stood motionless as the other fumbled with his belt. Adams said, "Unless Lefty would like to try his luck." There was a dull thud as Smith's gunbelt hit the dirt floor.

Lefty let his breath out in a long sigh. "There'll be another time," he said. He dropped his gunbelt and moved to his horse. Mounted, the two men swung around and rode from town. Adams stood in the doorway and watched them out of sight.

At the edge of town, Smith called a halt and forced his shaky hands to roll and light a cigarette. Only after he had it lit did he speak. "That was a close one."

"Maybe."

"Maybe, hell! He coulda took the two of us without raisin' a sweat an' you know it." He took a long drag on his cigarette letting the smoke out in a billowing cloud. "Why didn't he? That's what I want to know."

Lefty had been considering the same question. "He don't want no trouble in town," he decided reasonably. "No more'n Colter does."

The other pondered Lefty's answer for a moment. "Yeah, that makes sense," he said finally. "You think that was really Yates up on that ledge?"

"It weren't Santa Claus, that's fer sure."

"I don't know, he sure had some presents for the boys." His own nervous snicker spoiled the joke. "If he an' his boys are in this, an' Crawford an' Kirkshaw, they're goin' to have one hell of a tough crew."

"That's right," Lefty said noncommittally.

"I don't like it. That means Indian fightin' for sure."

"What d'ya' think we been gettin'?"

"Nothin' like we will get. You ever seen Pappy

147

throw a knife?"

"Hell, I never even seen Pappy."

"He can put a knife into a playing card at fifty feet." The thought brought back his nervousness and he glanced farefully over his shoulder, his tongue busy on his lips again. "Damned if I come up here to fight 'Paches. I want to do that, I'll go back to Arizona an' dig me some gold. I know where there's a whole creek full. Trouble is, there's 'Paches all 'round." He sent his cigarette arching out into the dark. "It could of been Pappy up there. He was with Adams in that business down south. You goin' to stick around for that kind of fightin'?"

Lefty shrugged. "It's what we're bein' paid fer."

"Not enough. Not for this kind of fightin'. I'll take that kind of chance for a gold mine or somethin', but not for wages. Know what I'm goin' to do? I'm stayin' in town tonight an' tomorrow I'm headin' back for Arizona."

Lefty shrugged again. "Suit yourself."

"Why not come along? Nothin' here but trouble."

"Where ya' headin'?"

"Phoenix."

"Fer how long?"

"Couple weeks."

"Maybe I'll see ya' there. I'm goin' to see how everythin' shapes up here first."

"Okay, see you 'round," Smith said in casual farewell. He started to rein his horse around toward town.

Lefty said, "What about your things?"

"The hell with them. I ain't ridin' back there for a blanket an' a razor, an' I got no money comin'."

Chapter 19

Dawn was only an hour away when Adams reached camp. Will was up already and there was a pot of coffee steaming among the embers of the fire. Frank shook the water from his hat and slicker and crouched down to hold his hands to the warmth.

"Coffee?" Will asked.

"Thanks. I can sure use it." He was in good spirits. Will noticed it and asked, "Good news from town?"

Adams considered the question as he blew gently on the boiling hot coffee. "Can't decide," he said at last. He told Will what he had learned from Martinson.

"I reckon it's good, considering. We had to figure he would get in some replacements, but the more that quit the harder it'll be to get them."

"I hope you're right."

"I'm right. Can't be too many around who'll want to fill in for somebody who found the going too tough. Hiring guns ain't as easy as it was eight, ten years ago. Unless Colter can pay through the nose, which he can't, he won't keep getting them."

Frank rolled into his blankets and was asleep in seconds. Nothing had been planned for that day, both the men and horses needed rest too badly, and he had expected to sleep until he was slept out. He was surprised when, five hours later, it seemed more like five minutes, he was awakened by a hand of his shoulder. It was Hartong. "Company coming," the foreman said "Rustlers if I'm not mistaken."

Frank slipped into his boots and followed Hartong along the rain softened floor of the canyon in which they were camped, to a point where it joined, at right angles, another canyon which was beginning to fan out to lose itself in Benton's Valley proper. Just short of the junction, they climbed the high bank to where Sarge was kneeling behind a line of boulders.

"Afternoon," Sarge said laconically. "Looks like we got company." He nodded toward a spot a quarter of a mile down the valley. Three riders were pushing twenty odd head of cattle in their direction.

"Ours?" Frank asked.

Sarge's answer was to hand over the glasses he had been using. Frank focused them on the herd and was able to read the brands. All but one bore the Lazy M. Lowering the glasses he asked, "Where are the others?"

"Howie and Paul are in the rocks on the other side. Johnny and George are up the canyon by those cedars. The rest are still on guard, just in case." Sarge's voice was a near whisper as the herd drew close. The low pitched whistling of one of the rustlers and the sharp creaking of saddle leather was clearly audible over the thudding hoofs.

Soon the lead steers began to amble past. A moment later the two flanking riders arrived. The rocks no longer screened the watchers, and the nearer rider, glancing up, looked squarely into the muzzle of a leveled rifle. His whistle broke off in mid note with a sharp intake of breath. The other looked quickly toward him, then to the top of the bank.

They both froze, the sudden tension on the reins bringing their mounts to an uncertain halt. For a second they hung poised between fight and surrender. Then they saw the others and knew how surely they were trapped. Slowly their hands went up.

The drag rider must have been blood brother to the gunman in the windmill yard. He displayed the same instinctive reaction to danger. The instant the others stiffened in their saddles, he pulled his pony around hard and raked it soundly with his spurs. Before his companion's hands had reached shoulder height, he was tearing down the valley at full speed.

No one said much as they returned to camp with their prisoners. They were just beginning to realize what would have to come next. They were in no position to turn these men over to the sheriff, yet they could not release them. Nobody cared to mention the alternative. Johnny and Nieman stayed in their saddles. The others dismounted. Hartong crossed to the cave and lifted the coffee pot from the still smoldering embers. Lescout stood beside the horses, looking down and drawing aimless circles in the soft dirt with the toe of his boot. Howie began drying the barrel of his rifle with a kerchief.

One of the rustlers looked around him then, with a shrug, swung down and walked over to the base of the canyon wall. No one stopped him. Squatting down, he pulled out the makings and began a cigarette. He was a dark skinned Mexican, quite

151

handsome, and quite a dandy, too, with a small, carefully trimmed mustache drawn out at the ends and waxed to dagger points, and black hair brushed to a high sheen. His clothes were flamboyant, but of fine quality, especially the hand tooled, leather boots and the pearl gray stetson with its band of black leather filigreed with silver. He was a picture of flashy elegance.

By comparison, his companion was drab and dirty. A heavy set man of forty with sandy hair and a florid face, molded by deep lines into a fixed expression of resentment. He kept his seat for several seconds then, seeing no one was paying any attention to him, shifted his weight to his left stirrup and started to dismount. He stopped abruptly and settled back as Lescout said, "Hell," and walked over to his horse.

Lifting the rope from the saddle, Lescout took two strides toward the fire. "Hartong," he said. The foreman wheeled to look at him. He made a motion with the rope. "We're going to have to move out soon." His meaning was clear.

For ten endless seconds Hartong hesitated. Then he said, "You're right." He reached out for the rope. "I'll handle it." Although he had been in charge for two weeks, no one had considered Adams in this. Cattle were involved which made it the foreman's responsibility. Hartong accepted it as such. His belated glance at Frank was only to consider a possible objection.

Frank hesitated, too. It seemed odd that after two weeks of killing, there should be such an aversion to this, yet it was strong in all of them. His answer was a slow, reluctant nod. It was a silent knell of doom for the rustlers, who took it in opposite ways. A slight twitch of the hand holding the cigarette, spilling a few grains of tobacco to the ground, was the only indication that the Mexician understood.

The other was of a different metal. The color drained from his ruddy face and his whole body began to tremble. He was a man who had lived every minute of his life in complete self indulgence, without consideration of anyone or anything. If he had ever had thoughts of possible capture or punishment, it had been the realm of fantasy; picturing himself making brilliant and daring escapes. Now he was faced with a reality he was not ready for. His mind went numb. None of the clever plans came to it. There was only a driving need to run.

He called out, "No," in a strangled half scream and drove his spurs into the flanks of his horse. As it exploded forward, he reached out and, more by luck than skill, yanked Johnny's Winchester from its boot.

Leaning forward he sent his big roan straight for the high bank at the end of the canyon. It was a fifty foot dirt slope, and a forty-five degree angle; an impossible route under any conditions. With the surface softened by hours of rain, not even the deer that had cut a zigzag path across its face would have tried it. His fear crazed mind saw it as a path to safety. He drove his mount straight at it. That the roan managed to scramble a third of the way to the top was remarkable. Then the surface began to slide out from under it like a rug on a waxed floor.

Kicking free of the stirrups, the rider came back down the bank in a stumbling run, firing his captured rifle in a flurry of useless shots. He didn't see them as that. His mind had created another fantasy for him. He saw himself fighting his way through a host of enemies to escape on foot. He died there, at the foot of the slope, believing that he was succeeding.

The Mexican had not moved from the base of the wall during the shooting. Now he straightened up and walked across to stand above the body. He stared down at it for a minute, then silently crossed himself and turned away. He stoped at the fire which Will was rekindling under the coffee pot. "A cup of that would set pretty well right now," he said. There was only a hint of accent in his liquid voice.

He took the cup Will gave him with a hand that was steadier than Will's and said "Gracias." His use of the

Spanish was habit. With "si" and "Senor," it was a word he had found he was expected to use, as though, somehow, they were all needed to prove an ancestry claimed by every line of his face. From the corner of his eye, he saw Lescout pick up the rope and walk with it to where Adams and Hartong were standing. Suddenly he had difficulty forcing the coffee past a throat gone tight and dry.

Kelly moved up to the other side of Adams, his eyes on the rustler, squatting by the fire. "Too bad. He's a good man in a lot o' ways."

"You know him?" Hartong asked curiously.

"No, but I've heard about him. What he was doing with those trash, I don't know."

"That's the trouble, we do know," Lescout said without humor. "Rustling."

"That's true. But he shouldn't have been doing it with coyotes like them. From what I hear, he's a man to ride the river with."

"Yeah, pushing somebody else's cow ahead of him." Lescout's sarcasm was deliberate now.

"Okay, so he's a rustler. I'm just saying it's too bad, that's all."

Adams did not hear the rest of the argument. Kelly's words had given him an idea. Not the perfect answer, maybe, but he doubted if any except Lescout would raise serious objection. He was surprised, nevertheless, at how readily they embraced the idea. Even Paul's objection was as much for the record as anything. It wasn't easy to hang a man in the cold light of day, particularly when he had become an individual, a person.

Taking the rope from Lescout, he walked over to where the Mexican still squatted, warming icy hands with the coffee he could not drink. The man did not look up as Adams reached him, but he could see the boots come to a stop in a rough half circle in front of him. Then the coiled and knotted rope struck the ground between his feet. His first reaction was fear, followed by anger at the callousness of the act, then

154

by hope. He had been studying these men. Callousness was out of character. There had to be something else. Tearing his almost hypnotized gaze from the noose, he lifted it to the faces above him.

Frank said bluntly, "We're in no position to turn you over to the law, you see that."

The rustler jerked his head in a short nod.

"And we can hardly let you go."

Another nod.

"Can you think of anything other than that?" Frank gestured toward the rope.

The rustler decided to try his voice and managed to keep it level as he said, "No, Senor."

"Your partner found one."

"He thought he saw a chance."

Frank shook his head. "No. He came apart at the seams, and you know it. He didn't have a chance in a hundred."

"Not one in a thousand," the other acknowledged. "He was a strange man, Senor. He dreamed of doing the impossible with ease, but he could not even do the simple things well." With a rare insight, he added, "He probably died without knowing he had no chance."

He waited then, stiff and tense, for Adams to speak his mind.

"All right, we'll give you a better chance than that. How much better I can't say. You know what we're up against, you can judge for yourself. You may be dead tomorrow."

"Senor," the man said with a touching dignity, "I am dead today. A dead man who sees even one more sunrise is very fortunate."

Adams nodded, less in agreement than in final decision. "Understand this. You'll get any dirty job that comes up. If there's any shooting, you'll be right up front."

The other's, "I understand," was tight and pinched with the backwash of fear.

"And you stick till this is over," Hartong warned grimly. He was coiling the rope over his arm. "We'll

155

still have this. You even look like you're trying to run out an' we'll use it.'

"I will stick," the rustler said.

Frank had his doubts, but only said, "All right."

Hartong said, "We better be moving out." He glanced at the sky and added, "Looks like we'll get a little more rain before the day's over."

"That's just ducky," Sarge growled. "We need it so bad."

Chapter 20

Just at noon, Stan Ard wheeled his wagon into State Street. He would have known the time without even seeing the big clock in Overmile's window. As he turned the corner, there were only half a dozen people on the street. Before he had gone half a block, the street was alive with hurrying figures as a score of clerks hit the sidewalks and headed, with determined haste, for the nearest restaurant. He felt a twinge of annoyance, having hoped to be in time to order his own lunch before the noon rush. He decided to have a beer instead, only to see four drivers come from the stage office and head for his favoriate bar. He wouldn't have admitted to being antisocial—he just hated crowds. If four men hardly constituted a crowd, they would tie up the barman, depriving Ard of half his pleasure in drinking; the opportunity to pour his troubles into the ear of a captive audience. He returned to State Street to pull in before Holman's store.

There were only two customers in the place, an elderly woman whom he didn't know, and his own nearest neighbor, Les Filepp. They were not close, but Ard liked Filepp as much as he did anyone and greeted him as cordially as his rather churlish nature allowed. Les looked up from the slip of paper he was reading, folded it casually and thrust it into his pocket, then extended his hand in a greeting so hearty Ard felt obligated to find something more to say. "What're you doin' in today?" he said. "Thought you damn near bought out the place last time."

"I damn near did, that's a fact. Still I forgot a couple of things. Salt for one. You'd be surprised how flat all that grub can taste without a little sale."

"Yeah, I guess." Small talk was difficult for Ard.

Not for Filepp, who continued easily, "That's not the worst. I forgot some thread Nancy wanted. A little spool of yellow thread like that," he held up thumb and forefinger an inch apart. "To hear Nancy tell it, I didn't bring nothing."

They talked for several minutes, Les carrying the weight of the conversation, while Ard made his purchases and carried them out to his wagon. Leaving Filepp there, he stopped by the Nugget and, happily, found the bar deserted. He pushed up to it and, for the next half hour, bent the unfortunate barman's ear. This unburdening of his troubles did not raise his spirits as it usually did, for he learned of the additional gunmen who had arrived without hearing of the several who had deserted. The news made his own future seem especially bleak. His tiny Wagon Wheel spread was now the only place north of Bear Creek; the natural boundary of the J.C. That it had never been part of Ed Barret's Hen Track would hardly stop Colter. Now, it seemed to Ard, nothing would. The thought put him in a depressed, self-pitying mood.

As he left the Nugget, he glanced up the street and saw Filepp's wagon coming from the alley beside Holman's store. It surprised him that Les would go back to the loading platform for the few purchases he had spoken of. The wagon turned away from him, heading out of town. Ten minutes later he was in his own rig, also heading out. He drove leisurely, so he was mildly surprised when, halfway home, he rounded a curve and saw the other wagon only a few hundred yards ahead. His immediate reaction was to slow down. Still in a black mood, he had no desire to catch the other driver.

Otherwise he thought nothing of it until he reached a point where the road crossed a small stream. He stopped to rest his team, deliberately taking a little extra time, and let his eyes sweep the far bank, where flood water had left a strip of soft earth. Few wagons had passed this way, and only one recently; the one just ahead. Its wheel marks were sharply etched in the moist earth.

He stared at them for half a minute, sensing something wrong. Twisting around, he looked over his shoulder at where the tracks entered the water, paralleling his own. There was no denying it, the other wheels had cut far more deeply into the soft ground. Yet his wagon and Filepp's were identical, so the other wagon was obviously fairly heavily laden.

There were several possible answers, including the chance that he was wrong about it being Filepp's wagon. Normally he would have shrugged off his puzzlement, but just now he welcomed anything which might divert his thoughts. There was one sure way to identify the rig ahead. He snapped the reins, urging his team up the bank, considering the problem as he drove.

Had Filepp's greeting been a little too hearty even for a friendly man? After all, they were not especially close. Then, too, the handshake had been held back until the scrap of paper, obviously a list, had been put away. It had been casual enough, but had it been natural? Had Les been too talkative in the following conversation, as though trying to divert his attention? The more he thought about it, the more certain he was that Les had been covering up. He was not one to take any great interest in his neighbors, but the minute someone tried to hide something from him, he became intensely curious.

His increased pace brought the other rig into sight again. He hung back, keeping pace with it, until it turned into the narrow lane leading only to his and Filepp's place. Ard turned into the drive himself and, five minutes later, came to a fork in the road. Here, above the left road, a three by four foot sign hung from the cross arm of a heavy post.

The sign was a result of his initial pride of ownership, before he discovered he lacked the ability and the luck—especially the latter, to become an important rancher on a shoestring start. He had brought the old maple table top all the way from Ohio for this purpose. He recalled how carefully he had laid it out, copying the letters from a specimen sheet begged from the local typographer. Laboriously he had painted in each character, checking the thickness of each upright, the length of each serif, willingly rubbing out anything which did not meet his demand for perfection. "The Wagon Wheel," it said, in bold letters, and underneath, "Stanley Ard, Proprietor."

It was pretentious considering what lay behind it, but it had expressed hopes and dreams which had never materialized. The post was canted sharply over under the sign's weight, and for the hundredth time he promised himself he would ride out and straighten it. For the dozenth time the futility of it struck him. How much longer would it be there anyway? A week? A month? Then some J.C. hand would tear it down to chop it into firewood. The thought brought back the bitter sense of defeat. Deliberately he pushed it from his mind by turning his thoughts to Filepp and his loaded wagon.

He had not thought beyond this point. Up to here, it had been just an interesting puzzle. If he followed further, he would be spying. Curiosity easily overcame any hesitancy on that score and he turned to the right. Half a mile up this fork, he pulled in behind a wall of brush at the foot of a low ridge. Swinging heavily from his seat, he climbed the ridge to a point from which he could watch Filepp's place.

It was small and neat, although Ard noted, with a certain jealous satisfaction, that the barn was badly in need of repair. Les was just closing the front gate as Ard reached the ridge top. Watching the wagon move up the drive toward the house, Ard wished for some glasses so that he could be sure of seeing what was unloaded.

He received a surprise as the wagon went up the slope past the barn, bumped heavily over the shallow ditch at the end of the drive, and pulled in behind the spring house. This building was wide and low, although not quite low enough for him to see what was being unloaded. That something was evidenced by the movement of Filepp's head and shoulders, visible across the roof, and by the lightness of the wagon as it bounced back down the slope. Les stopped in front of the barn and his boy came out to unhitch the team.

As the boy was leading it away, Les turned back to the slope and eyed the fringe of wood above the spring searchingly. The gesture crystallized all of Ard's thoughts. Les had driven into town for supplies, all right, but not for himself. Someone was to slip out of the woods and pick them up on the run. He did not have to be clairvoyant to know who it would be. The only questions were, when they would come and what use he could make of the information.

The answer to the latter came almost with the

answer to the puzzle itself. He was completely convinced that the Lazy M had no chance against Colter. With defeat certain, did it matter much whether it came today or tomorrow? If he was not really changing anything in the long run, didn't he have the right to think of his own interests? Even with the outcome certain, Colter would surely appreciate any help.

For five minutes conscience fought with self interest. It was an unequal struggle. Hurrying down the hillside to his wagon, he unhitched the team, gave one of the animals a sharp slap on the rump, and clambered on to the bare back of the other. Kicking it into a run, he headed toward the J.C.

Had Ben Dutcher still been foreman when Ard rode in, Colter's cattle empire might have been won that day. Tough and crude as he was, Ben was never consciously discourteous. Hippo Krale was of a different cut. He had a sadistic streak in him and he despised two bit ranchers like Ard, taking a malicious pleasure in belittling them.

He was not busy when the puncher poked his head into the office to tell him Ard was outside. He could have gone right out. Instead he said, "Tell him to wait. I'll be out in a minute." He crossed to his desk and splashed a shot of whiskey into a tumbler, then perched on the desk corner to watch Ard through the window. He grinned as he saw him tug uncomfortably at pants, soaked from crotch to shoetop with sweat from his saddleless horse. He still grinned as he watched the other shift nervously from foot to foot and glance uneasily at his door.

In his contempt for little people, it never occurred to Hippo that this one might be here to help rather than to ask for something. He chuckled as Ard reached for his tobacco, only to change his mind and shove the sack back into his pocket. Twice Ard started toward the main house, where Colter had been momentarily visible in a window, but each time he stopped after a few hesitant steps and returned to his

162

horse. Finally, with one last look at Hippo's door, he started for the house with a determined step that told Hippo he had stretched things as far as they would go.

Heaving himself up from the desk, Hippo moved to the door and opened it noisily, catching Ard in mid stride. He waited there, on the top step, as Ard looked guiltily over his shoulder, hesitated, then turned to walk back. As he approached, Hippo took out his own tobacco and began to roll a smoke. Looking down at the makings, he kept Ard waiting again. At last, the cigarette lighted, he looked up. "You wanted to see me?"

From that point on, Hippo moved as quickly as Dutcher would have. Yet he couldn't regain the minutes he had let slip past, and they were the difference between catching the Lazy M still loading at the spring house, with the chance of slipping in behind them, and having to charge at them across the open because they were already starting back into the woods.

The attack came as it had at the windmill; a dozen riders sweeping out of a hollow five hundred yards away, firing the minute they came into sight. This time the surprise was genuine, the Lazy M's momentary confusion unfeigned. They recovered quickly. Adams and Sarge swung to face the attackers, while the rest urged the pack horses into the brush.

The range was long even from standing mounts, but their first shots buzzed close enough to make the J.C. use precious seconds fanning out. Coming from the backs of running horses, the answering shots should have been hopelessly wild, but Lady Luck, who had smiled on them till now, had turned her back. One of the pack horses turned balky at the edge of the wood and refused to push into the tightly jpacked bushes. Nieman had to circle back and lash it on the rump with a coiled rope. The bullet caught him there.

Adams heard it hit and reconized the sound. He prayed a silent prayer that it would not be serious, but one glance showed that it was. Nieman was twisted around in the saddle, his weight all over on one side, one hand clutching the saddle horn, almost as though he had stopped in the act of dismounting. His other hand was pressed hard against his lower chest, and there was a puzzled expression on his face, as though he could not quite understand what had happened.

Frank and Sarge closed in on him, Frank taking the reins while Sarge held him upright. His face was chalk white and half paralyzed muscles tried desperately to pull air back into his lungs.

They pushed through the strip of second growth and into the heavier wood beyond. With Lescout and Kelly, Frank dropped down on the far edge of a level, grassy field in the hope that the J.C. would blunder out onto it. He didn't expect it, they had found a different type of pursuit to be safer. They would stick to it. Frank was not fooling himself, they were in a tough spot.

How bad it was depended a good deal on Nieman's condition. Leaving the other two on guard, he rode on to where George lay on a hastily made bed of coats. His shirt was open and Sarge was holding a heavy compress to his side, while Will tore a clean shirt into strips with his one hand and his teeth. There was little blood, and for an instant he took it as a good sign. One look at the other faces changed his mind.

He wanted to say something; to reach out to the man with some words of reassurance. He could think of none and, if he had, he felt they would not be welcomed by the rest. He was a stranger among them, his presence an intrusion, he had never felt this more acutely. He started to turn away when Nieman's voice stopped him. Glancing back he saw the man looking toward him. He dropped to one knee beside him.

Nieman's voice was quite clear, but each word was separated form the next by a painfully shallow breath. "It don't feel like it's too bad. I'll be okay soon's I get my breath. Soon's Will gits me patched up, I'll be able to ride."

Frank patted his shoulder awkwardly. "Don't worry about riding. This is probably the safest place we could spend the night, and come dark I'm taking ;you back to Filepp's. You'll be sleeping in a feather bed tonight."

Nieman said, "Thanks," and closed his eyes.

Adams stood up. "We can take him out the way we came in without much risk." He was not quite as sure as he tried to appear. "They'll be circling ahead now, not expecting..." He broke off, realizing that no one was listening. He turned back toward the man on the ground. He saw Will first, kneeling there, motionless, silent, a half torn strip of cloth dangling between his teeth and outstretched hand. Letting the end drop from his mouth, he wadded it up tightly in his tremendous fist, rose slowly to his feet and walked away.

That was the way Nieman died. Slipping away so quietly that only Will and Sarge heard the final sigh and, even at the end, not knowing how badly he had been hurt.

For the first time in his life Adams knew a sense of personal loss. He realized that it was only a shadow of what the others felt.

Chapter 21

If the days before the rain had been hard, those following Nieman's death were a nightmare. They twisted and dodged and ran, yet they were never able to break loose from the steady pursuit. It became a deadly game of hide and seek, with death as the penalty for mistakes. Twice they almost made them: once when they stayed on an established trail too long, paying for it with a pack horse and half their supplies, later when Steinholder was almost picked off as he skylighted himself crossing a ridge. The bullet cut a nasty gash across his shoulder.

The J.C. made its mistakes, too, getting a man badly wounded by cutting carelessly across the corner of a field at the foot of an innocent looking bluff. Both sides escaped worse than this a dozen times as much by luck as skill. Lady Luck was now turning a fickle eye on the Lazy M. One moment she saved them from an ambush, the next she blocked an escape route.

With each passing day their position was becoming more desperate. They were being ground down, driven to the point of exhaustion, and their horses were in worse shape. This time the sky gave no promise of rain. Worse yet, they had been forced into high country unfamiliar to any of them. They were following the top of a sixty foot clif, whose diminishing height and downward angle seemed to promise a return to the valley floor. It was a false promise. The cliff fell away until it was less than forty feet high, then began to angle upward again.

It was back to its full height when they came to the gorge. It was actually a beautiful sight. The stream, almost a river just now, came with dark and silent rush from the shadow of the canyon, to burst into cottony white as it took the first of its three plunges to the base of the cliff. Here it caught the sunlight and broke it and tossed it like gold dust to the wind. Halfway down a geyser of spray leaped up from the sharp edge of a boulder that split the stream, and in the mist above it hung a rainbow, arched like a Japanese bridge from bank to bank. They desperately needed a more substantial bridge. Its absence considerably dampened their appreciation of the canyon's beauty.

Now they had to turn to the left and somewhere to the left were the J.C. gunmen. Two hundred yards above the falls a narrow gully cut a path to the water's edge, but nature was being perverse. The opposite wall was almost vertical and glass smooth. Only a dozen yards upstream, the slick wall was finally broken by another gully. Had the two been reversed, they might have risked swimming. As it was, it was close and clearly unreachable. They followed the stream for half a mile without finding another break in the wall.

Suddenly they rode out of the timber and found another door closed in their face. They were at the foot of a treeless bluff, studded with boulders and cross scarred with rocky ledges. They could work their way up, but it would take time and they would be visible from miles away. Howie, riding in front, reined in and pursed his lips in a soft whistle. "Now that ain't even pretty," he said.

They drew up in a bunch and looked. "Even if it was I wouldn't like it," Lescout said, his voice grim. "If they should catch us in the middle..." he let the sentence hang.

"You think they got anybody at the top?" Kelly asked.

"If they know this part of the country."

There was a long silence, then the rustler, who had offered the name of Martine, said, "Senor?" They all swung around, surprised. It was the first word he had volunteered since giving them his name. "I have crossed that stream. Never when the water was so high as it is now. It would be very dangerous."

Adams looked up at the rocky slope. "More dangerous than that?"

"I do not know. I would think not."

Adams glanced questioningly at the others. Hartong said, "We got to try something." He swept his hand toward the hill. "And that sure don't look like a good bet."

Martine lead the way back to the first gully and down it to the water's edge. He looked at the rushing current apprehensively. "It is very high," he said softly. Frank realized, with some sympathy, that the man was deathly afraid of the water. There was a narrow gravel bar running a few feet in both directions from the gully. Martine pointed to the lower end and suggested, almost apologetically, "If someone would wait there with a rope?"

As Johnny rode in that direction, he turned upstream as far as the bar extended. Again he hesitated then, with a fatalistic shrug, he urged his reluctant mount in. Immediately he turned its head downstream and seemed to make no effort to swim it to the far bank. He was only a few feet out as he drifted back past them and had just reached midstream by the time he came to the lower end of the gravel beach where Johnny sat, rope in hand. There were straight walls on either side of him, here, without the slightest hint of a foothold.

It seemed to the watchers that the man must have been seized with a sudden urge to suicide and that only Johnny's rope could save him. Johnny, in fact, had started his loop circling for a throw when, two thirds of the way across, the horse came to a dead stop. The current was still sweeping by, but the horse was only turning in it. Suddenly it rose up in the water until its belly was barely touching the surface. Martine continued downstream until he had gotten in close to the far wall, before he turned and began inching back along the rock shelf that lay under the water.

This was the ticklish spot. He was out of reach of Johnny's rope and if his horse could not fight the current, or should stumble, he was lost. The sound of the falls was loud in their ears. At last he reached a point only slightly below them where a back eddy eased the pressure. He flashed a relieved grin across at them. "Do not try to swim too straight across, the current is too strong." He threw a double loop of rope around a spur of rock and added, "I will throw the rope and swing you in."

Adams acknowledged the instructions with a wave and said to the others, "I'll go first." The moment he felt the eager grip of the current, he understood the rustler's fear and, by the time the rope came to swing him in toward the hidden ledge, he could appreciate the courage it had taken to do this alone. One by one they made the crossing, inching back along the shelf to the gully mouth and up asked, his voice not unfriendly.

Martine's face was the picture of innocence. "I saw some cows crossing there one day. I followed them."

"And them cows knew all about that ledge?"

"Si. They were very smart cows." No one asked whose cattle they had been.

Chapter 22

They stopped in an aspen grove within sight of the gorge and unsadddled right there. Their horses were about played out and would not be in much better shape the next day. It left them with the same choice of evils they had been facing when the rains saved them. They could start with the first light and make a run for the valley, hoping the J.C. could not reform in time, or they could head for one of the passes above them and leave the valley.

They discussed it well into night. Next morning

they saddled up and turned toward the high pass. It was a bitter decision. As though to prove it was the only one, however, toward mid morning they looked back to see a lilne of riders on the slopes well below them. The net was reforming.

An hour later they entered an area familiar to Hartong, who had hunted it with an Indian guide, Joe Lightfoot, whose place was a few miles further on. Hartong took the lead and presently they were riding along the shore of a narrow, crystal clear lake. Lightfoot's camp was on the far side, near the lower end. The steady ringing of an axe on wood broke off as they drew near and, an instant later, Joe appeared on the far shore to lift his hand in friendly greeting. They returned the salute, but kept riding and had gone nearly a hundred yards when something clicked in Adams' mind. He pulled up so sharply that Sarge's horse practically climbed the back of his own.

He stared back toward the opposite shore, at a big birch bark canoe drawn up on the beach a few feet from where Joe was just turning back to his work. The germ of an idea became a full fledged plan. He shot rapid fire questions at Hartong. The answers produced an excitement that quickly transmitted itself to the others.

Without waiting for Frank to finish his questions, Sarge said, "It'll work, damn it. It'll work."

"You're damn right it will," Howie said. "It's a cinch, only two stretches of bad water, maybe a mile all told."

"Will Joe do it?" Frank asked.

"Hell yes! And enjoy it, too, if I know him."

Frank's gaze went the rounds of the group and found approval in every face. Even Johnny seemed to share the general enthusiasm. "What have we got to lose?" he said.

That seemed to be the final word. Frank said, "All right. We won't want to leave any tracks into his place. Somebody's going to have to swim across." He let the sentence end on a questioning note and saw all their heads swing toward Howie, who said modestly, "You're lookin' at the best damn swimmer in the valley."

Sarge snorted loudly. "Swim hell. You just splash so much you get pushed along by your own waves."

"Hah, you can do better, I suppose?"

"Maybe not, but Doc Prentis'll beat you with one hand tied behind him."

"Yeah? Then how come I beat him last fall?"

"I often wonder," Sarge answered weakly.

Adams said, "That's going to be a mighty cold swim. Do you think we could get him over here?"

The sound of the axe had started up again. Sarge said, "Not a chance. He'd never hear us. Anyway he's got t' leave his camp lookin' like he was out fishin' or somethin'."

"Don't worry about it," Howie said. "I've swum in colder water than this. There was ice formin' on the edges when me and Doc had our race."

Sarge seized the opening. "Sure, that's it. Doc broke through the ice and got stuck. You dove off the edge. Gave you a forty yard lead in a fifty yard race. At that, you only won by half a foot."

"You go to hell," Howie said cheerfully and swung a looping right that landed with a meaty smack on Sarge's shoulder.

Sarge gave a loud, "Ooooow, my arm! Ooooow, I think it's broke. Ooooow, somebody catch me, I'm goin' to faint," and fell forward over the saddle horn.

They were like a bunch of kids on the last day of school. The abrupt change was amazing, especially since they would be exchanging safety and a chance to rest for further danger. Frank envied Martinson for his ability to command this kind of loyalty.

Stripped to the skin, Howie plunged into the chill water and started for the far shore with powerful strokes. The others rode on to the lower end of the lake where they watered their horses and waited for Howie and the canoe. Frank moved up beside Steinholder and said, "I want you to take the horses over the pass." He cut off any objection by adding quickly, "I want you to get that shoulder looked at for one thing, and another, you can ride back into town without being recognized."

"I guess you're right," Murry agreed reluctantly.

The canoe came into sight, Lightfoot paddling, Howie sitting in front wrapped in a bright red blanket. The guide was supposed to be nearing sixty-five. There was nothing in his unlined face, or quick, agile movements to prove it. He could easily have lied away ten years. Hartong raised his hand, palm outward, and intoned solemnly, "How."

The guide copied the gesture and said, "How," with equal solemnity. Then his face broke into a wide grin as he added, "You old pale face son of a bitch, good to see you." They shook hands warmly as Hartong introduced Adams.

"Did Howie tell you what we wanted?" Frank asked.

"Well, his teeth was making a lot of noise, but I think I got the drift. Shouldn't be no trouble."

Frank looked at the canoe dubiously. It was not as large as some of the big Indian war canoes he had seen up north, but it had been built to handle groups of four or five would-be hunters with their equipment, so it was wider and sturdier than some of these. "How many can you take?"

"Six. Seven maybe, if you sit small."

"We'll sit small."

Lightfoot hooked a thumb at Howie. "Him sit small? Ha! He came up here once. Every time he look at canoe, it turn over."

"Hell," Howie protested. "I fell in once, that's all. An' I still think you tipped me just to win that dollar."

"I win all right. I still got it, too."

"I bet you have. 'Long with all the others you cheat people out of."

"Sure. I keep it to give you a chance to win it back. Some day we may be out in desert. Only water for miles is in canteen. Then I bet you don't fall in. Maybe

173

you win—maybe."

Adams sent Kelly and Will along with the horses. "It's probably best to have more than one man take them. They've got to be out of sight on the other side before the J.C. reaches the pass."

Joe assured them that, except for the stretch Howie had mentioned, the water was smooth as glass. It was not long before Frank decided the description was open to challenge. Their craft sat low in the water and, to a man new to canoeing, the choppy waves seemed to rise higher than the gunnels, threatening to swamp them at any second. A queasiness in his stomach wasn't helped by the spray whipped back ito his face by the wind. His hands clamped themselves so tightly to the sides that he was sure they would have to be pried up.

The stretch of so called "bad" water—he was becoming convinced that any water that moved was bad—required two portages. The first was only three hundred yards, where the stream roared through a narrow canyon. They had one chance to look down on the kind of water they were bypassing. It was like looking into a boiling caldron. The choppy waves leaped and cavorted like ballet dancers gone mad, turning the water a milky white with their own energy. No one remarked on its beauty.

They paddled a short run of genuinely quiet water, then disembarked on the far side to begin the second portage. Adams let his eyes sweep along the stretch of river they still had to pass. It did not look bad from here, but he wasn't fooled. He knew now what the crisscross streaks of white meant and saw how the spray leaped up along the rock lined shore.

Far below, a railroad trestle spanned the V of the canyon. The moment he noticed it, he noticed, also, a smudge of black smoke in the distance. Before the smoke had moved an inch along the horizon, he had another plan working. Again it needed only the right answers. "Does that train cross the bridge down there?"

174

"Reckon it better," Sarge said. "'Less it growed wings, that's the only track."

"Would it stop for us if we flagged it down?"

"Sure. That's the afternoon freight. McFarrin's the engineman on that run. He knows most of us."

Frank swung to Lightfoot. "Will we get down there in time to stop it?"

"No." It was flat, unequivocating. Frank felt like a small boy who had just had his candy snatched away. He paused uncertainly, not knowing what to say next.

"Not if we go around this," the guide said. "We can make it if we stick to the river." All eyes swung that way, all had the same thought behind them. Reading them he said, "It's not so bad. The part we just passed is the worst. I've been over both five, six times, and Howie's a good man to have up front."

Howie puffed up with pride at the compliment. "There's nothin' to it. Just close your eyes an' pretend you're in a rockin' chair."

Adams' stomach was churning again at the very thought. He left the decision to the others and caught himself half hoping they would say no.

Hartong broke the silence. "If it works, we could end the whole thing?"

"It might," Adams said.

As though that ended all possible argument, Hartong turned and started back toward the canoe. The others followed.

Everything is relative. Before they had gone a dozen yards, Frank was willing to accept the "smooth as glass" description of the upper river. It seemed as though they had mounted a bucking horse. Not an ordinary one, but an untamed giant with a wild and wicked strength which their own could never match.

They dropped down into troughs so low that the water on each side was like the walls of a vise threatening to close in on them. Then they shot upward and outward into nothing, to hang suspended for an eternity before crashing down with a force that drove Frank's stomach down into his boot tops, and

175

seemed sure to smash the bottom out of their frail craft. Boulders rushed at them like locomotives until, finally, he closed his eyes and was unashamed of his fear. He lost track of distance, of direction, of time.

Then, of a sudden, they rose out of a trough and did not come down again. He waited for the shock to come and when it didn't, tension built up within him until he wrenched his eyes open as the lesser of evils. They were gliding along a smooth dark flow of water. The trestle was almost directly ahead and there was no white water in sight.

They stepped ashore in the shadow of the bridge. Hartong looked back at the angry water and let his long held breath out in a sudden gust. Lescout began to work the stiffness from his fingers, and Sarge made an elaborate production of kissing the ground. Howie looked up from helping empty the water from the canoe and said innocently, "If anybody missed any of the sights, we'll be glad to take 'em through again."

Sarge looked at Hartong, who nodded. They sidled up beside Howie. Before he realized what they were up to, each had him by one arm and one leg and were swinging him between them, counting as they did. They had reached a count of two when Lightfoot said, "Train's coming."

They let Howie fall where he was, in two feet of water, and scrambled up the steep embankment. They reached the tracks just as the engine nosed into sight around a curve. The engineman thrust his head out of the cab window to study them then, recognizing them, let the train chuff to a stop. Looking down he said, ostensibly to his fireman, "Now ain't this a scurvy, lot o' train robbers?"

The fireman crossed to the top step and spat a long steam of tobacco juice neatly between Sarge and Howie, "Sure are, and not enough brains in the lot to see we ain't pullin' no express car."

"That's right. Ye boys'll not get a farthin' out o' this job, ye know."

"The hell we won't," Howie said. "We got this all

figured. We're goin' to knock you on the head an' pull all the gold out of your teeth. We figure to be able to retire for life."

McFarrin roared with laughter, flashing a set of gold fillings which almost justified Howie's optimism. "I wouldn't mind that as much as t' have ye tell the super I picked ye up. That could cost me me job."

They settled down on a flat car near enough the front of the train for most of the sooty smoke to pass above their heads. Frank had a chance to explain the new plan. Originally it had been to stick to the river until they neared town, pick up fresh horses and slip back into the hills. It would have been a blow to the J.C.. He could almost see their faces when they learned they had shut the door behind a quarry that had never used it.

Now luck had given them a chance to do far more. Even with the wide circle they were making, they were moving fast enough to put them ahead of the returning J.C. riders who, for the first time since the ambush at the mill, might be caught fully off guard. They could be hit harder, both physically and psychologically, than they ever could again. The question was where?

Frank considered every suggestion before voicing his own thoughts. "The odds are three to one they'll come back along the creek as Howie figures. I don't think that's good enough odds for a chance like this. There's only one place we can be absolutely sure they'll ride—into their own front yard.

Hartong and Lescout nodded, they had had the same idea. Sarge was doubtful. "You think we can do it? They keep a pretty tight guard on the place."

"A week ago, yes. But for the last five days they've known just where we were and didn't want to lose us. You can be damn sure every man who could ride was out after us. That means only the cripples and the cook are left, and maybe not even the cook. The problem is the horses. You're sure we can get them from Kinder's place without any trouble? We can't

177

afford to lose any time."

"Absolutely," Hartong said. "He's a friend of Dave's and Jim Pierce was his best friend. He blames Colter for that. He'll probably want to ride with us."

Frank nodded. This, he thought, was probably what would beat Colter in the end. He was buying his help, they were having it offered gratis. Martinson had been wrong about his friends, they were just a little slow in getting started, although Kinder would have let them have horses before if they had dared to run the risk of Colter discovering it.

They left the train at a farm little more than a mile from Kinder's place. The farmer had only one horse which he had to unhitch from the plow before they could use it. There was a stony silence when Adams asked for a volunteer to ride it to Kinder's. These were working cowhands. The idea of riding a harness scarred plow horse into a ranch was about as inviting as another ride down Wildman's Creek.

Finally, without a word of any kind, Johnny walked across to the horse, swung up onto its back, and rode off.

Chapter 23

The sun was turning a copper red when they finished their reconnaissance of the J.C. headquartes. Not unexpectedly, they noticed little activity. Only two men were in sight; a blacksmith, more audible than visible, working at his forge, and a guard with a bandaged head leaning against the corner of the corral. The latter appeared reasonably alert, keeping his eyes swinging around the three quarter circle of his range of vision and, every few minutes, moving down to where he could give the slope behind the house a casual once over.

In twenty minutes of watching they saw only two others. The cook appeared briefly to draw a bucket of water from the well and a man with a crutch hobbled to the outhouse and back. Adams said, "We better get moving. We could blow this whole thing by wasting too much time." To Lescout and Martine he said, "Give us five minutes before you ride in. You're just a couple of gun hands looking for a soft berth, remember. Don't try to get the drop on the guard until you're sure we're behind him."

"If he should wonder about those brands," Hartong said, nodding toward their horses, "you come in by train and bought them in town. At Roeders, he handles Harv's stuff."

The plan worked with ridiculous ease. The guard, secure in the belief that they were well back in the hills, gave his attention to the approaching riders. While he did, Adams and the others slipped down the hillside behind the house. Even on foot it wasn't easy, and they were acutely conscious of their exposed position every inch of the way. They breathed easier when they reached the house and found it emply.

With Hartong covering them from there, Sarge and Howie went after the cook, Adams and Johnny, the blacksmith. The cook caused no trouble. He had just cracked an egg against the edge of a bowl when Howie stepped through the door and Sarge appeared in the window. He threw a glance at the rifle in the corner and saw it was impossible. Mechanically he continued separating the egg and said, "Chow's at six, boys."

"Not tonight," Sarge said.

"I reckon not," the cook sighed.

The blacksmith was not as smart. He was holding a red hot iron bar in one hand and a four pound hammer in the other. For a second he froze, then he threw the bar at Johnny and tried to cut Adams in half with the hammer. He missed both. Johnny dropped him with a sledging blow of his gun barrel.

They took a minute to check the barn, then turn their attention to the bunkhouse. They had no way of knowing how many men they might find. Several obviously. The sound of an oddly mismatched trio emanated from there. A nasal tenor and a rich baritone fought it out with a timberless "whatzit" voice never squarely on pitch, to the notes of a well played guitar. The loser was "The Little Mohee." An occasional laugh cut through this, showing the total to be at least half a dozen.

Sarge and Howie eased through the back door, into

the room that had been Dutcher's, found it empty, and stationed themselves at the connecting door. Adams slid along the side of the building to the front corner, where he was only twenty feet behind the guard, still talking to Lescout and Martine. Martine saw him and said conversationally, "Here we go." He dropped his reins and wheeled toward the bunkhouse.

The guard said, "What the...?" and stopped as Lescout's gun came up to cover him.

"Don't be a hero," Lescout murmured softly.

Adams handed a shotgun to Martine and they pushed through the door. The guitarist saw them first, breaking off his play in mid note. The voices trailed on for a dozen words before coming to separate stops as Howie and Sarge stepped through the connecting door.

Frank said matter of factly, "Don't make any quick moves and no one will get hurt." No one moved at all.

There were seven of them, all injured to some degree. With the cook, blacksmith and guard, they had ten prisoners. The guard was sent back to his post—with an empty rifle and the absolute conviction that the first false move would bring a load of buckshot from the house.

Adams stayed in the bunkhouse with three men. The others took up posts in the house, barn and cook shack. They had barely reached their places when Sarge called, "Rider comin'."

Frank moved to the window where he could see the arrival, a tall man on a big gray horse. "Know him?"

"I know that gray. "It's one of their regular mounts."

"Probably coming on ahead to have the cook get busy."

As he drew near, the newcomer lifted his hand in casual greeting to the guard at the far end of the corral. The latter returned it, actually in answer to the unseen, but not forgotten, shotgun. The rider looped his reins over the rack and breezed into the bunkhouse. He had gotten ten feet into the room and had said, "I got news..." when his voice and stride broke together. He stared around the room as though he couldn't believe his eyes, then blinked hard in the apparent hope it was an illusion. "I'll be damned," he said. He paid no attention, except to step forward, when Sarge lifted his Colt and prodded him in the back with it. Suddenly he seemed to find something amusing in the situation. He managed a wry chuckle and said again, "I'll be damned."

Again they settled down to wait, only to become aware of the unnatural stillness. "It's too damn quiet," Sarge said. "If the cook was gettin' chow, there'd be some noise from there. We better have Johnny kick a few pans around."

Howie said, "We're too quiet, too." He picked up the guitar and held it out to the man who had been playing. "How about a tune, fella?"

The man looked up at him for a full second, then spat at his feet. "Go to hell," he said.

Howie shrugged and turned away.

"I don't think he likes you, Howie," Sarge taunted.

Frank held out his hand. "Let me see it, Howie."

Howie passed it to him, but couldn't quite hide his surprise when Frank tucked it under his arm and began to pick out a tune. Frank's thoughts turned bitter. Did they always have to be surprised whenever he did anything but shoot? What was it that kept him apart? Not just his reputation. Less than two weeks ago they had been ready to hang a man for rustling. Yet now he was accepted as one of them while Frank was still an outsider.

Sarge, who may have sensed something of his mood, helped some, saying, "Hey! he not only plays, he plays good."

He wasn't trying to play well, only loudly. Loudly enough to be heard by any approaching riders.

Ten minutes passed. Fifteen. The pressure was building. If the man on the gray had been the advance rider, then the rest were due soon. Adams wondered if something could have gone wrong. Could they have suspected something and even now be slipping in as the Lazy M had an hour before? He knew the others were thinking the same thing and were ready.

Another five minutes crept by while nerves drew tighter. Then Howie's voice came, showing the strain in spite of his effort to be casual. "Here they come." They were the same words, spoken in the same tone, that had been used on the first day. It struck Adams as prophetic; as though things had gone full cycle and, as that was the beginning, this was the end.

They came over a low hill and angled down to the river, riding heavily, tired, and without caution. Martine thumbed back the hammers of the shotgun and said to the men on the floor, "Turn on your faces and lie still." He hefted the gun suggestively. "Do not give me reason to use this."

Adams kept his fingers plucking the guitar strings. Howie added a rhythm with a knife handle against the top of a clothes locker. They watched the riders turn into the road and rattle across the bridge. The leaders entered the narrow passage between the corral and the branding pens.

Courage is found in unexpected places. The men on the floor lay stilll under the shotgun's threat, but one of the men on the beds, so badly wounded it was agony to move, let his hand slip over the edge to grip a boot top. With a violent effort he brought it up over his head and sent it crashing through the window. He stared, eyes round with fear, as the shotgun came around, but Martine had lost interest in him, swinging instead to the lamp, to crush out its flame with his hat.

Half the riders had entered the space between the fences before the warning came. Almost before the sound died, the hidden guns opened up, turning the area into a riot of rearing, screaming horses, and shouting, swearing riders fighting to get clear. The near darkness and the boiling violence of the action made it impossible to pick targets. They merely laid a withering fire into the heart of the frenzied mass until their rifles were empty.

They were using the same pattern; hit and run. As soon as he squeezed off his last shot, Adams shouted, "That's it." No one hesitated. Some of the J.C. had gotten clear and were beginning to return the fire in earnest.

At the door, Frank drew his Colt and fired two quick shots into the wall just above the prone figures, dropping a lifting head back to the floor with an audible thump. As he turned to leave, the guitar caught his eye and, on impulse, he grabbed it. They mounted up and, keeping the bunkhouse between themselves and the J.C. crew, rode around the mess shack. As they reached it there was an explosive whoosh and the kitchen burst into orange flame with a violence that shattered its windows and drove Johnny, who had just taken a running step from the door, to his knees. He jumped up unhurt and scrambled into the saddle.

They spurred for the darkening shadows of the woods. Behind them the doorways of the barn were turning a flickering amber and two windows of the house were touched with the same telltale hue. The J.C. was going to be busy.

In spite of that certainty, they followed a twisted, zigzag trail which would have shaken off pursuers in any case. Full darkness found them in a stand of pine only a mile from the J.C.. They could have safely made their campfire as bright as any of the three clearly visible from the ridge behind them, but the habit of caution was strong. Sarge built a tiny, shielded fire and began to brew coffee.

Adams climbed to the ridge top with Hartong to view the havoc. The barn was a pillar of flame, climbing skyward on a ladder of crimson sparks. No effort had been made to save it, or the mess hall which was blazing as fiercely, although its tin roof forced the flames out to the sides like the opening blossom of some squat flower.

A score of tiny figures, proof positive that there had been no pursuit, were fighting to bring the third blaze under control and to keep it from spreading to the bunkhouse. The J.C. had been hurt more than in all the other assaults combined. They had been caught believing that it was all over but the shouting, and had been hit harder than ever. More important, the Lazy M had done it without losing a man. This was the key, the heart of their plan; to make the J.C. feel that they were fighting a phantom, a will-o'-the-wisp which they could not really hurt. A dozen men had been lost in trying, yet the phantom was still there, somewhere, ready to hit again. If the J.C. was tough enough to take this latest blow, they could take anything. Adams didn't think they were.

He accepted a cup of coffee from Sarge, took a couple of careful sips, then set the cup down and reached behind him for the "borrowed" guitar. Between sips he tuned it. With the first twanging note, a dozen eyes swung toward him. Howie said, a distinct pleasure in his voice, "Hey, you brought it with you. How about playin' somthin'?"

Frank took another swallow of coffee and settled himself. He caressed the strings with gentle fingers, drawing a sound that died amid the voices of the wind stirred trees before it had gone fifty feet. He played the old, familiar tunes; the night herder songs, the trail songs, the war songs, but with a rare and sensitive musicianship that touched them all. They settled down to listen, finding in the music an easing of tensions a way to forget death and violence. No one spoke. Each listened in his own way, thought his own thoughts. The fire burned down to a few red coals, and overhead, fluffy clouds in endless supply scurried across the face of the moon.

Chapter 24

The beginning of the end of Colter's private army came with shocking suddenness. One minute he was riding through the early dusk, considering how to consolidate a victory, the next he was seeing his plans blown apart in an explosion of gunfire and flame. After that there was nothing he could do to hold his crew together. Three men left next morning. Others drifted away through the next two days until there were only seven able bodied men left. These were staying only on the assurance that Hippo would be back on Wednesday with a new bunch.

"He better bring in a dozen top men," their spokeman stated flatly. "Otherwise we've had enough."

"He will," Colter answered positively.

Hippo had been less sure. "That's damn little time. Goin' to be hard to find good men short of Dodge or Kinsley."

"We don't have time. Half the crew's quit already."

"That's the trouble. Nobody's anxious to fill the

shoes of somebody what found the goin' too tough."

"They will if we pay enough. Offer what ever you have to. Just get that crew. I'll meet you in town Wednesday." Colter had still been confident then. Later, sitting in the office, the least damaged part of the house, he stared into the cold fireplace and wondered. He wondered, too, where he had made his mistakes.

Sending for Adams had been one. Everything else had gone as expected. He was a good judge of men. He had figured Starbuck right. He had known just which way Martinson would jump. He had weighed Oncina and the Hazels and found them weak. But he had taken Adams on reputation, which was letting someone else do his judging for him. Still it had been a bad break. He had offered the gunman an honest proposition, he was capable of thinking of a killing in these terms, at a damn good price.

That Adams hadn't accepted had surprised him, but there had been no argument, no hard feelings. Just a business proposition—offered and rejected. Why had he stayed on? More important, why had he thrown in with an underdog outfit like the Lazy M with the odds so much against them? He gave a brittle laugh as he thought of the odds. How easily they had been changed. Now he was on the short end.

That had been another mistake. He had underestimated what Adams would mean to the Lazy M and had let them bring the fight to him. They had done so with a vengeance, half winning it before he realized he was in danger. He shook himself out of his moody reverie. He was doing himself no good with this kind of thinking. He wasn't finished yet. When Hippo got back with a new crew, things would be different, no business as usual while the Lazy M chose the time and the place, no attempts to wear them down with a steady pessure. He would use their own methods. He thought he knew how.

The Thull brothers were back in town. They were old time hunters who kept the town supplied with

187

fresh game. No one living knew the high hills as they did. It should be easy for them to locate the Lazy camp. He would keep his men out of it until they did. Then, with them to show they way, he could slip in and finish this. The thought restored his confidence. He had one drink of brandy and turned in for a sound night's sleep.

Approaching town an Wednesday, he lost some of his optimism. He knew the town had all the details of the debacle, although he hoped they didn't realize the six men riding with him was virtually all he had left. He guessed they did and the thought agered him. He straightened in his saddle and rode past their curious gaze with an air of cool detachment. Behind this facade lay a burning desire to get the Thull brothers on the job; to meet Hippo and to ride back through town with a score of guns behind him.

He found the Thulls butchering a deer behind the market. Sam wiped his bloody hands on a flour sack apron, more red than white now, and listened to Mark's offer. Jed remained squatting down, casually whetting his knife on his boot top.

"So you'll give us a hundred just to locate Adams and his bunch for you?" Sam repeated unnecessarily.

"That's what I said."

"Yeah, you did. What do you say, Jeb?"

Jeb lifted his shoulders in an elaborate shrug.

Turning back to Colter, Sam said, "Okay, we'll do it. How 'bout a double eagle to seal the bargain?"

Mark hesitated. The Thull's reputation for honesty was hardly good. Finally he reached into his pocket and pulled out the coin. He tossed it to Sam, who hefted it a few times, then asked, "Worth another if we tell you where they are right now?"

Mark felt a thrill of excitement. The freshly killed deer spoke of a recent hunting trip. They could easily have run into something. Without a word he dug into his pocket for another coin and tossed it after the first.

Sam caught it deftly and the faint smile that had

been touching his thick lips broke into a derisive grin. "You want to know where the Lazy M bunch is? Why they're eatin' chow in the Palace dinnin' room just 'bout now."

"The Palace! Here in town?"

"Why the Palace is still in town, ain't it Jeb?"

"Last I heard," Jeb answered.

Colter was swept by a blinding anger. "You sons of bitches," he said. Spinning on his heel, he stalked off, forgetting, in his anger, that he would need these men.

Sam's voice followed to remind him. "If you lose them again, come on back."

That he had been taken for forty dollars was a minor item. That the Lazy M had the gall to come openly into town as though the fight was all over was the thing that rankled, excluding for a moment any thought of personal danger. Halfway across State Street, he heard his name called. Looking up, he saw Dave Martinson on the walk ahead. What stopped him short, however, was the sight of Frank Adams a few feet to the rancher's right. Unconsciously he took a backward step and glanced around, hoping to see some of his own men, or even the marshal.

Frank thought, "He isn't as good as Dutcher."

Still Mark managed to show more annoyance than fear in his answering, "Yes?"

"We'd like a word with you if you got a minute," the rancher said. "At the bank in, say, ten minutes?"

The mildness of the tone brought Mark's courage flooding back. "I've got nothing to talk to you about."

"But we got something to say to you, and you got nothing to lose by listening. Vogler's office in ten minutes?"

Adams pushed away from the wall. The move brought his hand an inch from his gun. The threat was unintentional, but effective. Mark said, "All right, ten minutes," and turned up the street. With every step, the question, "What could they want," raced through his mind.

Finally it occured to him that they either did not know how badly he had been hurt, or believed, as he did, that it was only a temporary setback, making this their best chance to bargain. The thought took the edge off his temper. He approached the meeting with a certain anticipation. He was surprised to see his own attorney, Sam Goss, as well as Vogler in the latter's office. "What the hell are you doing here, Sam," he demanded.

"Just looking after your interests, my boy." Sam spoke with a false heartiness that disturbed Mark. No one was acting the way he sould. "I went over the papers while we were waiting," Goss continued, he seemed a little nervous. "Everything is all right. A little unusual, but perfectly legal."

"Papers? What papers? What's this all about, anyway?"

Goss looked at the others. "You haven't told him?"

"Damn it! told me what?" Mark exploded.

Motioning to one of the empty chairs, Vogler said, "Sit down, Mark, this will only take a minute." The banker eased himself into his own chair behind the big walnut desk. He was a stocky little man with a layer of fat that suggested softness—at first glance. Those who knew him, knew different. He picked up several papers from the desk and passed them to Colter. "These are what we are referring to."

Mark accepted the papers, but made no effort to read them. "And just what are they?"

"Briefly, Mark, the first empowers the directors of this bank to sell the land, the cattle and all other tangible assets of the J.C. ranch at public sale and..."

He got no further. Mark left his seat as though stung. "Sell the J.C.! Are you crazy? What is this, some kind of joke?"

"No joke, Mark," Vogler said calmly.

"Just what," Colter said with what he hoped was biting sarcasm, "makes you think I'd sell the J.C.?" There was a growing hollowness in his stomach. This wasn't quite what he had expected.

Vogler shrugged. "I don't think you have much choice."

His calmness shook Mark. He couldn't bring the sarcasm back to his voice as he asked, "Just how do you figure that?"

"Because you're through." It was Martinson speaking. There was a harsh bite to his voice now. "Some of the boys took over your place ten minutes after you left. They didn't have to fire a shot either."

It hit Colter hard. He had been sure they wouldn't hit the place again. At least not so soon. And some of the men who had been left there, while unable to ride, had been perfectly able to fight. Everyone seemed to have lost his guts all of a sudden.

Martinson's voice cut into his thoughts again. "The Hazle Brothers joined us yesterday. They're picking up all the leather you've got around and moving all the saddle stock that they can locate."

This was the other barrel. With Hippo bringing a new crew in by train, he would need at least a dozen saddles and twice that many horses. It would cost a fortune, and there probably wasn't that much leather in town.

With an effort he ordered his thoughts. It wasn't as bad as it sounded. Some of the men would bring their saddles and there was plenty of second hand stuff around. It would just take a little rummaging around to locate it. Nor would the horses be a real problem, they could hardly move all his stuff. No, if this was the worst they had for him, he was all right. It would set him back a few days, that was all.

He let a contemptuous sneer twist his lips. "I figured you for a bunch of damn horse thieves. This just proves it."

"Horse thieves or land thieves, what's the difference?" Martinson snapped.

"I'll tell you the difference," Colter snapped back. "We hang horse thieves where I come from. And that's just what I'm going to do; run down the bunch of you and hang you up like shirts on a line, if I have to

191

hire a hundred men to do it."

Adams smiled faintly and Mark detected a hint of mockery. "What will you pay them with?"

Mark felt like a man fighting blindfolded. No matter what way he turned, he was hit from an unexpected direction.

Vogler picked up another paper from his desk and said, "Yes, that brings up another point, your note. In the past, renewal was automatic so you may not have noticed that it hasn't been this year. It was deliberately delayed due to the uncertainty of the situation. In the light of recent events, we will not be able to renew."

"Hell, the J.C. is worth ten times that note. Any bank in the country would loan me that."

"Perhaps, but you took this loan out when you first came here. The specified collateral is your original holding; the Bear Creek land and buildings. With the buildings lost, we feel the value is insufficient to cover the note. Of course you may apply for a new note with the entire property as collateral. I'm sure the directors will consider it carefully. Otherwise, you have thirty days."

Before Mark could frame a sufficiently scathing reply, the banker added, "Considering the unusual circumstances, for the bank's protection, I have ordered that no money be released from your account until this note is met."

Mark went rigid in his chair. For a second he wondered if he could be hearing right. Could this be happening? Could it be legal? He doubted it. He looked toward Goss, but the lawyer kept his eyes focused on the carpet. Had he sold out, or been scared off? Suddenly he realized it didn't matter. Illegal though it probably was, there would be no time to challenge it.

Looking at the banker, Colter's anger flared out of control. "You crooked bastard! What are you getting out of this? How much did they pay you?"

Vogler remained completely unruffled. "I'm only

192

interested in the bank and the town. I can see neither of them benefited by a range war that is allowing rustlers to strip the range while it is being fought."

Before Mark could renew his tirade, Adams pulled a pair of crumpled yellow papers from his pocket, smoothed them out and shoved them toward him. "You're not going to need money anyway. Hippo isn't bringing anybody back with him tonight."

Colter picked up the telegrams in a daze. How could they even know what Hippo was doing, much less when he would be back?

Adams said, "They're from the boys who took the horses over the pass. They ran into him in San Luis. Even signed on with him." The telegrams told the rest. The first told of Hippo's effort to hire a crew, the second, of its virtual break up when news reached it of the present crew's condition.

The blows had been delivered with a calculated timing that left Colter groggy. He was like a man on a carousel which had been steadily speeded up until he was bobbing like an apple on a string, and everything around him was a blur. And all the time there were the voices, of Adams, of Vogler, of Goss, of Martinson, urging him to sign.

He found himself actually holding the pen in his hand when he brought himself back to his senses. Things had happened too fast. He had to have a chance to think. Had they thrown things at him too suddenly? Had they been too insistent? Could it be that they had hoped to upset him so much that he would do something rash? Why hadn't they waited until Hippo returned to tell of his failure? Was it possible the telegrams were fake; that Hippo was actually bringing in a big crew?

Eagerly his mind caught up this last thought. This had to be the answer. Somehow they had heard that Hippo had rounded up a crew and had made this last desperate play. They had done it well, grudgingly he admitted that. But they must have been hard pressed to think he would fold that easily.

He managed a touch of mockery in his own voice as he said, "An interesting proposition, gentlemen. Not very tempting, I'm afraid." He stood up, relaxed now, confidence restored. "But if I should change my mind, I'll let you know."

"We'll be here," Adams said, denting the newborn confidence.

To Vogler, Mark said acidly, "I'll pay that damn note, but it's the last business I'll do with this bank."

"Your privilege," Vogler said.

A drink was plainly the first order of business, Colter decided, as he left the bank. However he deliberately passed the saloons that could be seen from the bank, waiting until he reached the Staghorn. He downed the drink as soon as it was placed on the bar and shoved the glass back for a refill. Confidence faded as new questions flooded his mind. For the next hour, he was on an emotional seesaw, going from deep depression to supreme confidence and back again.

A hundred times his eyes searched the horizon for a sign of Hippo's train. At last he saw it, a smudge of smoke clouding the clear sky. He hurried toward the station, realizing that his haste was obvious, but not able to slow his steps. Arriving ten minutes before the train, he found a place between the wall of the express office and a partly loaded express wagon where he could hide his nervous pacing.

If Hippo brought in enough men, he was in business. The money being tied up wouldn't be serious right away, he had enough cash for immediate expenses. The Lazy M would have to be eliminated fast, that was all. Once that was done, there were plenty of people to lend him money, even the bank probably—Vogler ws a businessman first. Or, with the price was up, he could market some beef.

The train panted up to the station like a tired hound and came to a clanking, groaning stop. The conductor swung down, set his portable step on the ground, and called, "Step down, step down." He reached up to assist two young ladies descend amid a swirl of skirts and petticoats to the shrill, excited greetings of a half dozen friends.

They were followed, more sedately, by an older woman, then a young father, who was almost knocked off his feet by charging offspring. A pair of drummers, sample cases under their arms, stepped down with practiced ease, and finally Hippo Krale.

Mark felt a quick excitement as Hippo was followed by a slim, dark man, whose two thonged down guns declared his calling. It died swiftly as the waiting passengers started to board the train.

Hippo said something to the other man, who nodded briefly and turned toward town. As soon as Hippo reached him, Mark said, "What happened? Where're the men?"

Krale's voice was dead tired. "There ain't any. Not yet anyway." He gestured toward the restaurant. "I ain't et since breakfast. Let's do our talkin' over there."

They found two stools at the far end of the counter and sat in silence while the waitress took Hippo's order and returned with a steaming bowl of soup. Hippo crumbled a handful of crackers into it and, leaning well forward so the spoon would have the shortest distance to travel, began eating noisily.

Between spoonfuls he told his story. "I went down the line as far as Pratton, stoppin' at every place worth callin' a town. It weren't easy. I had to offer top wages and I weren't gettin' top men. But I did get a fair bunch signed up. Then, just when we was ready to come back, some of the old bunch drifted in. Pete Sooner for one. Remember him?"

"A loud mouth bastard with no guts."

"That's right. Well, they started soundin' off about how tough it had got here. Laid it on thick. By the time they was through, you'd think they'd been up against the whole Comanche tribe and this guy Adams was a cross between Crazy Horse, Jim Bowie, Bill Hickok, and a couple of other guys you can name. Then a rumor got 'round that Pappy Yates and his brood was in this. Then a couple of the new bunch started soundin' off. Pretty soon there ain't a man willin' to come."

Hippo had time to finish his soup and get well started on a platter of roast beef while Mark expressed his pent up emotions in a long monologue covering thoroughly the moral fiber, probable parentage, physical appearance, and sexual proclivity of all hired gunmen.

Hippo nodded agreement. "You can't get top men in the places we been tryin'. Not the number we need, anyway. Maybe in Dodge or El Paso or someplace like that."

There it was again; the thought that somewhere else were the men that he needed. "I don't think so," he said roughly. "Those hired guns are all alike. Anyway, we don't have time." He described the meeting in Vogler's office.

Hippo tried to whistle around the edges of a bite of roast beef, but only succeeded in dribbling the gravy down his chin. He wiped his mouth with the back of his hand and said, "They were damn sure of themselves, weren't they? What really hurts is the money. What're you aimin' to do about that?"

It was more than an idle question. Hippo couldn't be scared off, but his loyalty lasted exactly as long as the money. Understanding this, Mark said, "Luckily I've got a fair account in the Hortonville bank that they can't touch. The big worry is a crew. Without it a million dollars wouldn't help." This wasn't an easy admission for Mark. The heart of his whole philosophy was the belief that money would buy anything.

"How many of the old bunch left?" Hippo asked.

"Six, that can ride. They'll be drifting when they hear you didn't bring in another bunch."

"Would they stay if I did?"

"They said so."

"Then we still got a chance. The bunch I rounded up

will still come in if we do one thing first."

"What?"

"Get rid of Adams."

"Hell, they don't want much, do they? Does he really make that much difference?"

"What do you think? Would you be in this spot if he didn't? Get rid of him and the rest'll fold like a wet noodle. You know that as good as me. So does the crew."

"Just how do you figure on getting rid of him?"

"There's only one way. We can't buy him, and we sure as hell can't scare him."

"I don't want another alley killing. I got blamed for one and it ruined me in this town."

"That's the truth! Fact is, Pierce done you more harm dead than alive. It would still be the surest way, but maybe not the best. We need somethin' to make us look good, which we ain't been lately. Now if he was to get killed in a stand up gun fight, nobody could get very sore, considerin' who he is. And havin' the man who done it on your payroll ain't goin' to hurt us none."

"Sure, but just who do we use? You said he could put three shots into you before you cleared leather."

Hippo shoved his empty plate back, wiped his greasy hands on his shirt and signaled for pie and coffee. "I thought maybe the Tucson Kid. I wanted you to use him against Pierce, remember, but you chose Adams. Can't say I blame you. He's good. Guess he's proved that. Still in a straight out gun fight, I think the kid would take him. Anyway that was him that come in on the train with me."

There was a pause while the waitress brought Krale's pie and coffee, and his appreciative eye followed her well proportioned figure coming and going. "You really think he's that good?" Mark asked.

Hippo waxed enthusiastic. "Boss, the Kid's a regular magician with a gun. Fastest I ever seen and I seen some fast ones in my time; Thompson, Earp, Ringo, and a sight better shot than some, too."

"Adams didn't get his rep by being slow."

"That's the truth. That's why I ain't promisin' nothin'. I'd put my money on the Kid, but I wouldn't give no odds. Nothin's sure in this sort of play except a bullet in the back."

There was another long pause, then Colter said, "If he fails, we're through. The crew won't stay another hour."

"That's right," Hippo said flatly. He thought he understood why Mark had lost while he, Hippo, would have won. Mark wouldn't play this game the way he played poker, but tried to copper all his bets instead. His plays had been too devious, too cautious. Hippo would have steam rollered over the opposition and the hell with what people thought. When Mark didn't say anything, Hippo asked, "You got any better idea?"

"No."

"You want to sell out?"

"Of course not."

"Okay, then this is it. Sure it's a gamble, but you don't have no choice. You got to get a crew, and damn fast. If this don't work, you're through, that's a fact. If it does, you rake in the whole pot. There'll be a hundred men beggin' to sign on before the week's over."

Colter considered Hippo's assessment and was forced to a reluctant agreement. Yet he hated to bet everything on no better than a fifty-fifty chance. He searched his mind for some way to improve the odds, and suddenly an idea came. He explained it to Hippo who shook his head doubtfully. "I don't think the Kid'll go for it. He ain't like most of them rep hunters. He's a prideful bastard."

"Why tell him?" Mark said. "If he loses, he'll never know. If he wins it won't matter."

Chapter 25

Adams had sensed what was in the air the second the Kid pushed through the swinging doors and swaggered up to a place at the other end of the bar. He had been a little over casual, had ignored Adams a little too pointedly. Others had sensed it, too, and had gradually eased away from the bar, leaving the two of them alone.

Frank felt the warning tingle along his spine. He had been here before; had watched a half dozen rep hunters strut up and start their play. The words were ifferent, but the pattern was always the same; the cocky arrogance; confident aggressiveness; the veiled innuendo, and the unveiled; the direct insult then, if necessary, the challenge.

The Kid had followed the pattern, changing nothing, adding nothing except, possibly stirred by the thought that he might be interrupted, he had rushed it a little. There had been others before him. A few Frank had managed to bluff, others he had talked out of it. Two had died. There would be only one way with this one. He knew that instantly, just as he knew how desperately he wanted to avoid it. He had never been like the Kid, enjoying the kill, relishing the reputation it built. This killing—he never doubted the outcome—would be a flat and tasteless thing, to be avoided if he could.

He took the Kid's insults with a calm and infuriating detachment. Where an answer was necessary, as to the Kid's sneering, "I'm talkin' t' you, mister," he kept his reply casual, noncommittal, returning the burden of the talk to the other with a soft, "I know." It was futile. The Kid kept pushing, his remarks becoming more barbed.

Finally Adams took another tack. "How much is he paying you, kid? Enough to kill a man, or maybe get killed?"

"He's payin' plenty," the Kid admitted easily. "But you know what? Now I think I'd of done it for nothin'. Just for kicks. Just t' see you tryin' t' squirm out of it."

"But what do you really get out of it? Colter makes a fortune. You just make yourself a target for every rep happy punk in the state. Every town you ride through will have one just dying to see if you're as good as your rep."

The Kid laughed. "Dyin' is right. Let 'em come, I'll take care of 'em. After a while they'll learn."

"That's what I thought," Adams said. "But there's always one more." Turning away, he pushed his empty mug toward the barman and began to talk to him as though the conversation with the Kid had ended.

The Kid was a man with a purpose. "You're talkin' to me, remember?" he said caustically. The bartender's hand shook as he flicked the foam from the mug and set it in front of Adams. He stepped away quickly, to busy himself with some bottles on the backbar. Frank lifted the beer and took a long swallow.

The Kid's voice hammered at him again. "You know what? I think you're yellow. I think you're so scared your pants are wet right now."

Adams stared at the beer in the mug; a tiny amber pool, encircled by a wide collar of white. There were two small bubbles in the center, looking like gladiators in an arena. He shook the mug slightly several times, but couldn't move them from the center.

"All right, Kid. I'm scared. I don't want to fight you. Why not let it go at that? You can walk out of here and tell everyone I didn't have the guts to face you, with witnesses to prove it. You'll be the man who showed me up. The man who made me beg. Why not be satisfied with that?"

For a second the Kid seemed to hesitate, and Frank added, "I'm going to finish my beer and walk out of here. Let's leave it at that."

Perhaps, with the last sentence, he had said too much, convincing the Kid of his fear; sharpening his desire to kill. Perhaps the Kid knew the calmness in his voice belied the admission and felt that the watchers sensed it also. More likely he had just gone too far to stop.

"The hell you are. You got t' go past me t' get out and you ain't got the guts. Because the first step you take I'm goin' t' kill you whether you go for your gun or not. I'll give you a choice, though. You can let 'em carry you out on a board, or you can crawl out on your belly." The Kid smiled, but there was nothing behind his curving lips but teeth.

There it was, all laid out. Kill or crawl. It was no

choice. He hoped the town would understand that. A bitter anger stirred in him. Just when it had seemed to be all finished, the fighting and killing ended, when it seemed that he might have an end to loneliness, this glory happy punk had come to threaten it. The thought broke the last ties holding back anger. Not enough to make him rush into anything. He was too old a hand for that.

Ignoring the Kid's heavily sarcastic, "Well how about it, MISTER Adams?" he studied the room in the bar mirror. There would be nothing behind him, no windows or doors and the two tables at that end of the room were empty.

There was only one man at the table that would be at his right. Both his hands were on it, the right one well forward and holding a shot glass. His right hip was pushed under the table edge so that his gun would be imposible to get quickly.

Frank started to swing his eyes away, then brought them back abruptly. There was something familiar about the man. The Kid's voice started in again, "Where did you get your rep, anyway..." but Frank pushed the sound into the background as he concentrated on this man. Then, suddenly, he had it. This was one of the men he had met in the barn. The one he had automatically nickmaned "Lefty." Being left handed, the man's gun hand was only inches from his gun.

Adams felt the tingle along his spine again, this time with a cold chill to it. He was whipsawed. As though to prove it, the man brought the glass to his lips, then set it down untouched. Frank saw how unnaturally far out on the table it was, as though trying to proclaim its harmlessness. At least he was warned. He had that much edge. He turned his attention back to the Kid, catching him in mid sentence, "...in the back. Or maybe you didn't even do it yourself. Maybe you had somebody else shoot 'em for you—from an alley."

His meaning was clear. Adams' anger welled up in

202

him now. A cold, vicious, deadly anger. The killer within took over. It showed in his eyes. The barman saw it. He moistened dry lips and pressed himself hard against the backbar. Frank wheeled away from the bar, taking a step back to bring the man at the table a little more into sight. His eyes stayed on the Kid, however. "All right, punk," he said softly, "make your play."

The Kid saw the killer too, not just in the eyes, but in the whole body, seemingly so relaxed, yet so completely ready. He felt a thrill of fear. But he was still confident. Again he smiled the smile that did not get beyond his lips. "I'll let you make the..." His voice went on for another two words without change in inflection, but it was here that he made his move. And he was good!

Yet there was three thousand hours of practice behind the gun he was trying to match. He did match it in speed, but he sacrificed a hairline of accuracy for speed, and the Nugget's bar was a long one—there was twenty-five feet between them.

His shot cut a long, bright scar in the edge of the bar an inch from Adams' left arm, just as Adams' shot slammed into him, spinning him half way around. Frank drove one more shot at him, saw it hit and, dropping to one knee, spun with desperate haste toward the gunman at the table.

If the Kid's mid-sentence move had not fooled Adams, it had completely fooled Lefty. He had half risen and his gun was fully out, but not yet clear of the table edge. He froze in this position as Adams' gun came into line, his intention made clear by every taut line of his body.

How he managed to stop his shot, Frank never knew. He would have said it was impossible. Somehow he kept his thumb from slipping off the hammer, and for a long moment they held motionless, a tense, deadly tableau. Then Frank's finger relaxed on the trigger.

Lefty swallowed the growing lump in his throat

and, with infinite care, swept his arm around until his pistol pointed away from Adams. Without a word he opened his fingers and let it clatter to the floor.

Very slowly Frank came to his feet. Lefty stood like a statue, left arm still held out as though reaching for something that was not there. "You got a horse outside?" Frank asked grimly.

The other gave a short, nervous jerk of his head.

"Get on it and keep going."

Lefty nodded again. Fear still rode him hard. He managed to keep his steps fairly steady as he crossed the floor, his boot heels striking like hammers in the heavy silence. Only his last three steps were hurried. He pushed through the doors, heard them slap together behind him and let his breath out in a quivering sigh. He ducked under the hitching rack and untied his horse. Swinging into the saddle, he spurred to a fast trot.

A block away the remnants of the J.C. crew stood on the walk and watched him approach. Pulling up in front of them, he looked down and said, "He weren't good enough."

"Dead?" one of them asked.

Lefty nodded.

"How?" the other asked. He had known the Kid and could not believe he had been beaten fairly.

"He started a play he couldn't finish, that's all. It were a fair fight."

"Where the hell were you all this time?"

"He had me spotted. I never had a chance. He could of killed me easy, and I ain't goin' to wait around to find out why he didn't."

He started to rein around when one of the others said, "Wait a while, I'll ride with you."

"You can catch up. I ain't givin' him no excuse to change his mind."

At the Staghorn bar, Hippo received the news with a stoical calm. Carrying his glass, he walked back to Colter, sitting in moody silence at a rear table. Without preamble he said, "Well that does it. The Kid

204

weren't good enough." He shook his head, not quite able to accept it. "Lefty folded. God! that Adams must be good. You picked the best, that's for sure." He grinned wryly, then went on, "'Less you thought of somethin' else, I reckon we're through. The crew is ridin' out now."

He waited a minute, but Mark didn't answer. "So I guess I'll be takin' my time, too."

Colter looked up and for an instant there was a bitter hatred in his glance. It faded quickly. After all, Hippo was just a wolf who ran with the pack, and there was no pack left. He pulled out his wallet and dropped some bills on the table.

Hippo pocketed the money, lifted his glass to his lips, and said, "See you 'round."

Chapter 26

Adams looked down at the Kid. Death had erased some of the hardness from the face, accenting the boyishness. It was a hell of a time to die, he thought. The Kid hadn't been much of a man, but then he hadn't had much of a chance to be. Adams felt a little sick. It must have shown. A hand nudged his elbow and, looking around, he found the barman holding out a shot of whiskey. He murmured, "Thanks," and downed it in a single gulp.

The doors swung open and the marshal pushed through. He saw the body on the floor and Adams standing at the bar and read the story at a glance. Instantly he was hostile, his face grimly angry. Before he could speak, Troy Beasley called, "Mac," and walked over to him.

When Troy had finished his low voiced conversation, the marshal looked at the others. "That the truth of it?"

One of the others said, "Absolutely, Mac," while Lovejoy added, "I couldn't have taken as much from the Kid. Adams did everything but crawl, but the kid wouldn't buy it."

"He had to earn his pay, too," the third man said.

"Pay?"

"Colter. The kid admitted it."

"I see." That virtually ended the matter as far as the marshal was concerned. He listened to Frank's story with understanding, if not with sympathy. Glancing down at Adams' arm, he said, "He nicked you, I see."

Frans said, "No," surprised, the felt the pain. He put his hand to it and brought it away wet with blood. "I'll be damned." Slipping off his coat, he saw the answer; a sliver of wood, sliced from the edge of the bar by the kid's bullet, had cut a jagged gash along his left forearm.

Lovejoy came over and said, "Let me see that.' He pulled out a clean handkerchief, soaked it with whiskey and tied it over the cut. "Looks nasty. Better have the Doc look at it when he gets back." Ever sensitive to the subtlest shades of expression, he read the glance that Adams threw at the Kid's blanket covered body. "Put it out of your mind. His destiny was a bullet, and he would have continued to kill until it came. The town will understand that."

Adams felt a surge of relief. If the important men in town accepted this, the rest would eventually follow suit. Lovejoy was an influential figure and he evidently spoke for Beasley.

The doors opened and Dave Martinson limped heavily across to Adams. "You okay?" he asked gruffly.

Frank nodded.

"This Mark's work?" When Frank nodded again, he said, "The bastard." He signaled for a beer, then added, "You planning to do anything about it?"

Adams managed a tired smile. "No. I can't blame him for trying. It was a big pot, and he still had one card left."

"Glad you see it that way."

"I think it was his last play. You might invite him to

another signing."

"He's through, all right. Hippo and the others just left. I'll send the boys with another invite." He looked up at Adams from under bushy gray eyebrows for several seconds, arrived at a decision and said, "Ann is over in the Palace lobby."

Frank grabbed his coat. "Why didn't you tell me before?"

Martinson gave him the same studied look. "I happen to like her very much," he said.

Ann rose from the red plush sofa and stepped toward him, stiff petticoats rustling faintly under a powder blue dress. "Are you all right?" she asked.

"Yes, I'm fine."

"Your arm?"

"Nothing serious, just a flying splinter."

"I'm glad of that." She led the way to one of the plush sofas, not the one where she had been waiting, but a secluded one in the corner of the stairs. Sitting down, she pulled her skirt aside so that he could share the seat. "It was pretty bad, wasn't it?" Her voice was softly sympathetic.

He had thought that he had his emotions under full control. Not against the warmth of her understanding. "I didn't want to do it," he said. "God knows I didn't want to."

Impulsively she took his hand, holding it tightly in her own. "I know that."

"We killed a dozen men out in the valley."

"That was a war. You were fighting for something that was right. And fighting for someone else, too. This was a senseless, useless death. I'm so happy that you wanted to avoid it."

"Was it enough to want to?"

"If there was nothing else you could do. I'm sure tht there wasn't."

She was right. He had seen the futility of it. Watching the Kid's sneering face, listening to his prodding voice, he had seen the ghosts of the others leaning over his shoulder, mimicking his gestures, echoing his words; the glory hunters, wanting a reputation so much they had been willing to die for it—and had. The senselessness of it had struck him, and it had seemed important not to add another to the list.

Ann's voice cut into his thoughts. "What will Mark do now?"

"He doesn't have much choice. He has neither the time nor the money to make another fight of it. With a note to pay off and a ranch to rebuild, he'd be hard pressed just to hold things together. I think he'd rather sell out."

"Then the fighting will be over?"

"I hope so."

"What will you do then?"

"That depends on Dave. If he wants to let our partnership stand, I'll try to help in rebuilding the Lazy M. If not I'll try to build the Chain Link into something, maybe with Paul and Murry. Either way I'm gong to stay here."

"I hoped so much that you would."

It was said with the straightforward sincerity that was so characteristically her that a question slipped out he had barely dreamed of asking. "Could you marry a gunfighter, Ann?"

"No. But I could marry an exgunfighter. And if that is a proposal, the answer is yes."

For once in his life he did the right thing at the right time. He kissed her. Them time got away from them. Before they knew it an hour had passed as they talked and planned. They were interrupted when Dave Martinson appeared around the angle of the stairway and dropped heavily into the chair opposite them. He massaged his injured leg gently. "Been walking too much," he said. He looked at them for a second, excitement animating his face. "Well, it's all over."

"Over?"

"Yep. Colter came in on his own and signed every paper. Got to give the devil his due, he took it good; no whining, no trying to bargain. Just said, 'I lost big

209

hands before.'" The rancher shook his head slowly. "I can't believe it. Damn me, I can't believe it. I didn't think we had a ghost of a chance after the ranch was lost, he had such a big crew."

"A crew's only part of it. He never had the solid base under it. That takes twenty or thirty years of building; the credit no one thinks of questioning, the political connections that reach all the way to the state capital, the social position that makes everyone want to hobnob with him. He was moving too fast too soon. I thought we had a chance to chop him down, if we could stay out of his reach while we did it."

"Well, you did it. Damned if I understand how, but you did. Now the work begins. We got to rebuild the ranch and work cattle at the same time."

Frank pulled out his watch, snapped open the lid and began fumbling for the key. "I'm going to let you off the hook on that partnership, Dave. I'll take back the Chain..."

Martinson silenced him with a gesture. "I'm no hypocrite, Frank. We both know why I accepted your offer, and I'll admit that as little as a week ago I'd of been glad to of had you let me off. But I been talking to the boys and every one of them says they'd be proud to ride for you. That's good enough for me, since I'd 'bout decided the same thing. So if you think you can put up with an old fool who don't know enough to come in out of the rain, I'd be proud to have you with me." He held out his hand. "What do you say?"

Troubled and unpleasant dreams, in which he saw the Kid again and again, kept Adams awake until nearly dawn. When he finally did sleep, it was as though he had been drugged. It was past noon when he finally roused himself enough to make his way down to the dining room. Tho noon rush was over, but he found Martinson just starting dessert. The rancher stayed with him as he ate. When they left, they found Martine waiting on the porch. "The trouble is all over now, Senor Adams?"

"Yes, thank God," Frank answered.

"Then you will not be needing me any longer?"

"No. We could use you, though, if you want to stay on."

"I appreciate that, Senor, but I think I will ride on."

"Your privilege. The job's yours if you want it. You've more than earned it."

"Thank you, but my brother has asked me many times to join him in the freight business. I think now that I will. There are no cows there to tempt a man." He hesitated a moment, then added, "There is one thing, Senor."

"Yes?"

"Last week some of the crew were talking of the killing of Senor Pierce, here in town, and wondering who had done it. Some still blamed the J.C. in spite of what Senor Dutcher said. Others thought the rustlers he had trailed the week before had done it. I do not know if Senor Dutcher spoke the truth, I do know it was not the rustlers."

Martinel had been staring out into the street, eyes following a passing rider. Now he looked directly at Adams and continued in his soft, precise English, "I was one of them. It was Blake, the one who escaped, who fired at Senor Pierce. We were certain that he had not seen us, so we had no reason to fear him. Nor were any of us in town that day. We were...busy elsewhere. I thought you would want to know."

"Thanks, I'm glad you told me," Adams said. The question of Pierce's killer had been in the back of his mind since it had happened, pushed there by the pressure of events, but not completely forgotten. Now it took a front seat and stayed there through the rest of the day.

He was leaving the Palace dining room after supper, when he saw Dan Prentis crossing the street toward the Nugget. They met at the door and went in together. Prentis looked tired and, as he took his bag, the barman said, "Tough day, Doc?"

Prentis nodded. "Freight wagon turned over down the line. Driver's leg broken in three places." He closed his eyes and took a deep breath. "You work all afternoon, then wonder whether a man will ever walk again."

"He will, if you fixed him up, Doc," the barman said.

"Thanks," the Doctor said. Finishing his drink, he said to Adams, "Better come over and let me take a look at that arm. It's the kind of thing that gets infected easily."

"Just going to ask you to."

They crossed to the Doctor's office. Prentis put his bag on his desk and said, "Give me a few minutes to clean up, I'm a mess. He went into the back room and, presently, Frank could hear water splashing.

He stood by the front window, looking out into the street. Across the way he saw the hitching rail where he had been standing when Jim Pierce had died. Looking up the street, he could see the corner Pierce had rounded and, in his mind, he could see Pierce turn the corner and walk toward him. As he visualized it, a wagon swung in from the middle of the street and pulled up in front of the general store, blocking his line of sight. With a sigh he turned from the window.

Prentis' bag lay on the desk. He snapped it open and found it as jammed as doctor's bags were reputed to be. He wasn't surprised to see the short barrelled, five shot revolver tucked down into a side pocket. Many doctors carried one, although it was a standing joke that they wouldn't be able to find it if they need it. The sound of splashing had ceased, and a dresser drawer had opened in the other room, when he slid the gun back. He walked to the door and called a couple of youngsters away from their game of marbles. A quarter sent them racing away on an errand for him.

A minute later Prentis stepped from the other room, buttoning a fresh shirt and looking like a different man. "That's better," he said. "Now let's have a look at that arm."

He had just finished the bandaging when Marshal MacDonald knocked and entered. He gave Prentis a friendly greeting, then said to Adams, "You wanted to see me?"

Frank nodded. "I was wondering if you had gotten anywhere with Pierce's murder."

"'Fraid not. And with Colter and his crew gone, I don't guess I will."

'You think it was one of them?"

"Can't say that, got no proof. Seems likely, though."

"Dutcher claims it wasn't," Adams said and told the marshal about his meeting with Ben.

"Why didn't you tell me this before?" MacDonald asked, his tone a little sharp.

"Sorry. Guess it slipped my mind. We were kind of busy."

"Guess you were at that. It isn't likely Ben would lie. 'Less, of course, he did it himself. He took quite a beating in that fight."

"Was he the kind to get even from an alley?"

"Hell no! At least I'd sure of bet against it. But then you can't always tell."

"No, you can't," Frank agreed.

"What of those rustlers he had the trouble with?" Prentis asked. "Some people think it might have been them."

"Could be," the marshal said, "but it doesn't fit good. Not enough reason. If he didn't see them, it didn't matter. If he did, he wouldn't have kept it a secret, so it wouldn't have helped them to kill him."

"I have assurance that they didn't," Adams said.

"Martine?" MacDonald asked.

"Yes. Just this afternoon."

"You didn't call the marshal over here just to tell him that," Prentis said. "You've got another idea, don't you?"

"Yes. I know who did it," Adams said bluntly. He saw the marshal stiffen in his chair. "I should have known long ago. So should the marshal. Trouble is, I didn't know the people well enough, he knew them too well."

"Who?" Prentis asked. His voice was a perfect blend

of expectancy and doubt.

"You," Frank answered calmly.

The Doctor's face was a mask of astonishment, with just a hint of a, "you must be joking, but I don't get it," expression. It was this last that he put into words. "You can't be srious." Like the expression, the tone was perfect.

"I am though."

"Just how do you figure it?" There was amused tolerance in the voice now.

"Because it couldn't have been anyone else. That's what I should have seen before. I stood right across the street and watched that wagoner take his team through the cross alley. He couldn't have more than reached the other end when Pierce came around the corner. Yet he didn't see anyone. And you came along the only other route, and saw no one. Where was the killer? He didn't have time to come behind you, or you would have heard him."

The Doctor laughed easily. "Hell, friend, don't hang me that easily. There are a dozen places a man can hide back there."

"Yes, but why? He couldn't know just when Pierce would come down the street, so how could he know when to break from a hiding place to be there when Pierce arrived?"

"I admit I can't answer that." Again the tone ws just right. "I only know it did hapen, so it had to be possible."

"Possible, but not likely. Add enough unlikely things together and it gets hard to accept."

"Just what other unlikely things do you have?" Prentis' tone indicated he thought the joke had gone far enough.

"You said you were hanging up your coat, looked out and saw Pierce come around the corner and walk toward me. Marshal, will you look out and see if you can see the corner?"

Without moving, the marshal said, "You can see the corner all right from here." There was a touch of anger in his voice. Prentis was a friend, Adams was not.

"Will you try anyway?"

MacDonald shrugged and went to the window. "I can't see now because of that wagon, but..." he broke off and turned to look at Prentis, uncertainty showing for the first time.

"And there was one there then, too," the Doctor finished for him. He was still poised, but a little grim now. "It was far enough up so I could see past its tail."

"No," Adams said. "It was in the same spot. It was going to be unloaded the next morning, it would have been as near the door as possible."

"The driver wouldn't have worried about that," Prentis scoffed. "He didn't have to unload it. Anyway, Mac checked my story."

"Not then. By the time he had questioned me and checked the alley, it was dark. Next morning the wagon was gone."

"What else do you have?" MacDonald asked.

"His own actions for one. The time element for another. He saw a man shot down on the street, yet instead of going out to see if he could help, he went the other way, after the killer. But he didn't chase him, just went to the back door, a matter of one minute, two at the most, yet it was better than five minutes before he came out front. Then he was suddenly concerned about Pierce even though he was told, by people who had been there five minutes, that he was dead."

"A doctor can hardly take a layman's word about something like that," Prentis said. "He has to make sure."

"But you didn't. You knelt down, carelessly getting quite a bit of blood on your pants, put your hand on his shirt for half a second, then went to help Miss Holman. Again you didn't act like a doctor. Here was a woman in a state of shock; a close friend needing attention, yet you stood there and gave your life history. Not just clearing me, a dozen words would have done that. You told where you have been, when you got back, what you were doing when the shots were fired and what you did afterward."

"You're probably right, there," Prentis said. "But don't you think I might have been a little upset, too?"

"I'll bet you were."

MacDonald said, "What do you say made the time difference?"

"My shot. It barely nicked him, but it was enough to put him in a bad spot. There he was with a bullet torn coat and a bloody shirt, not knowing whether anyone knew he was in his office, wondering if they would decide to bring the body in here and find him that way. He had to get rid of the coat and shirt in a hurry. When he had, he found it was only a gash. A simple compress, maybe a towel held in place with a couple of turns of court plaster, would stop the bleeding."

Frank looked at Prentis in near sympathy. "That couple of minutes must have been hell, Doc, thinking that any second someone might come in and catch you. But no one did, and once you got another shirt and coat on, all you had to do was take your nerve in your hands and walk out into the crowd. You hadn't had time to check the rest of your clothes for blood, so you knelt down beside Pierce. That way any blood stains would be taken for his."

"How did he get from here to the alley in time if he didn't see Jim at the corner?"

"He wasn't in here at all. He never comes here first when he gets back from a late call. He goes straight to the Nugget. It's a ritual. The barman automatically takes his bag and puts it behind the bar. That's where he was headed when he saw me across the street and Pierce coming around the corner. There, while we were watching each other like hawks, was a perfect chance. Simple and apparently foolproof."

"Plan a murder and carry it out in thirty seconds? That's a little hard to believe," MacDonald said dubiously.

"If you hate a man enough to kill him, then you've

216

thought about it. It's not too big a step from thinking to doing, if the chance comes. This was a perfect chance, and Doc's no stranger to quick decisions."

Prentis dropped a roll of bandage into his bag, picked up a pair of scissors and leveled them at Adams. "Just why am I supposed to have hated Jim?"

"Margaret Holman. You loved her, but she chose Pierce. It's not the first time a man's been killed because of that."

The marshal said, "You got any proof of all this?"

Frank asked, "Who's the best swimmer in town?"

MacDonald looked puzzled. "Doc, I guess."

"And the most enthusiastic, too," Adams agreed. "The first one in every year, last one to quit. Yet a week after Pierce's death, they couldn't get him into the water for love nor money. Why? Because he couldn't hide the bullet scar. There'll be a hundred witnesses who'll testify that it wasn't there before."

The Doctor looked down at the scissors he was holding then dropped them into his bag. When his hand reappeared, it was holding a gun. "I knew it would come apart. There were too many holes." He spoke without malice, but the agony of mind and soul, so long hidden, lay bare now. "I didn't really hate Jim. I just loved Margaret enough to do anything for her. I never thought of Jim being killed, though, until Mark told me he was bringing you in." He saw Frank's sudden interest. "Surprised that he would tell me his plans? I was part of them. He asked me to spread that rumor about Ed Barret dying before Sarah.

"Oh, it was probably true, all right. I was willing to say so in town, but I couldn't have sworn to it in court. Anyway, that's when Mark let me in on his plans. It sounded good, Jim out of the way while I had nothing to do with it. I began to have new hope. But you refused the job. I was there just after you left, and Mark didn't know how he was going to handle Jim. I think if I hated anyone, it was you.

"Then Jim came down the street and I saw another chance. I'm sorry I did. I was sorry the second I shot."

217

He sounded sincere even though he was obviously talking to mark time while he made quick, desperate plans.

Now he ordered them to drop their gun belts to the floor and kick them under the leather couch. The marshal seemed ready to resist, but recognized the tense determination behind the leveled gun and compiled with an angry gesture.

Perhaps subconsciously, Prentis had foreseen this day. Without taking his eyes from them, yet with a minimum of groping, he found another satchel and filled it with trays of instruments from the case beside him and some personal things from the desk drawers. He was working against time. Any second someone might step through the door behind him. A minute later he snapped the case closed and, with a motion of the gun, ordered them into the back room. They heard the key turn in the lock, and the Doctor's rapid steps across the floor, followed by the violent slamming of the front door.

Instantly MacDonald hurled himself at the connecting door. Frank turned and made a more leisurely inspection of the narrow rear window. The lower sash had been nailed shut, but the upper one was free. He lowered the sash and leaned out. By twisting around he could catch the top of the window frame with the tips of his fingers and pulled himself out.

The door must have been more sturdy than it looked. He was able to drop to the ground, reenter through the back door, and turn the key in the lock, before the marshal's assault produced more than a half inch split in one panel. MacDonald came charging through like a rampaging bull. At the front door he stopped and gave a brief, but impressive, display of his vocabulary, ending with "...the son of a bitch took my horse, too."

In spite of himself, Adams laughed. "You shouldn't have ridden when you could have walked, Marshal. He was supposed to take mine."

For an instant the implication escaped MacDonald, then he whirled on Adams. "Supposed to! You mean you let him get away?" Anger followed surprise. "You better have a damn good reason, mister. Pierce was my friend. I don't go for you letting his killer escape even if you did expose him."

The acid anger in his voice sobered Adams. "Come back in, Marshal. It's nearly dark. You won't be able to do anything tonight." He waited until the marshal had closed the door again. "I don't know how good my reasons are. I didn't know Pierce. Maybe if I had, they wouldn't seem as good to me. As it is I'm more concerned with the living than the dead, Margaret Holman in particular. What's it going to do to her if she finds out, just now especially, that he was killed by someone else she is fond of—and because of her?"

This was his strongest argument and he saw that it had a tempering effect on the marshal's anger. He continued, "She would be hurt most, but a lot of others would be hurt, too. People who trusted and respected him. Hell, some of their children are named after him. It would tear the town apart.

"Maybe I don't have the respect for the law I should have, though it's increased a lot since I came here." A little honey wouldn't hurt, he thought. "As I see it, laws are made to protect a community, not to hurt it. If a law doesn't work, or enforcing it will hurt too many people, it's changed.

"Trouble is, in this case, just bringing it out into the open will do the damage. And believe me, it will be damage. I know what things like this do to a town. I don't want to see it happen here. I figured I had only two choices, forget about it and let him get away with it, or just let him get away. I hope I made the best choice, but I'm sure it was better then letting the town be torn apart with an arrest and trial."

This was his case and he was smart enough to rest it there. He waited quietly while MacDonald considered it. Anger was gone from the other's voice when he said, "You got a good point there, Adams, but towns have survived things like this before."

"Not without being hurt."

"That's true, but we can't let murderers get away scot-free just because somebody else might get hurt."

"Not somebody, Marshal, everybody. And Prentis won't be getting off scot-free. You see, he's not a good murderer. He has a conscience. If it were Hippo, or the Kid, it would be different. They don't have his respect for life. They would kill again without hesitation and forget it as easily. Prentis will carry it with him as long as he lives, and there will be times when he will wonder if he can live with it. To tell the truth, I don't think he can."

Frank saw that he had made an impression and pressed his advantage. "You can't make the decision, of course. Your job is clear cut. Why not take it to Judge Holman and the rest of the town council? Let them decide. It can't be kept a secret indefinitely, but the longer it can, the better."

The marshal looked out at the darkening street. "Maybe that would be best. Couldn't do much tonight.' It was a welcome chance to pass on the responsibility. As he recovered their guns from under the couch, he added, "You took a chance letting him get that gun, or didn't you figure on that?"

"I thought of it." Reaching into his pocket, Frank brought out three shells and dropped them on the desk.

MacDonald looked down at them. "Three?"

"There wasn't one under the hammer, and I left the last one in case he wanted it."

"I hope he uses it," the marshal said bitterly. "Seems to me there was a hell of a lot of crimes committed around here without anybody being punished."

"Maybe, but it's only in novels that all the loose ends are all neatly tied up. In life some of the worst get off while some of the best pay. Anyway, they didn't all get off. The Kid is dead. He was the worst. Colter started it with his compulsion to own more, and will be lucky to salvage fifty cents on the dollar. He'll spend the next ten years thinking of what might have been. As for Dan Prentis; he's carrying a burden of guilt, not to speak of fear, I wouldn't take for anything."

"I reckon that's so," MacDonald said. As they left the doctor's office and started across the street, he added, "You got to give him one thing, he didn't try to hang it on you. He could have done it easy that first day." He had taken only a few steps before he caught the fallacy. "That wasn't to help you, though, was it? He couldn't be sure nobody else had seen where the shots had come from."

Frank nodded. "And to explain the time element." he said. "That was his big problem, to keep anyone from wondering why he had taken so long. That's why he said so much when he did come out, and that was a mistake."

"How's that?"

"He made two or three positive statements about things he couldn't have been absolutely sure of. It was out of character."

"That's right, by God. I never thought of it."

"Neither did I until a little while ago. That's when I first began to wonder about him."

They reached the far walk where Troy Beasley and Joe White were standing. Troy said, "Didn't I see Dan Prentis ridin' out on your bronc, Mac?"

For a second the marshal hesitated, then said, "Yes. Got word of some epidemic over around Two Rivers. I let him take my nag so he could go over the pass."

"That's jus' like Doc. Ride all night so's he kin break his back for a week curin' people he never seen a'fore. An' if'n he gits ten bucks from the lot, he'll be lucky."

"Yeah, there ain't many like him," White said reverently. MacDonald's look at Adams

221

acknowledged defeat.

As they approached the hotel, Frank's heart gave a sudden leap. Ann Holman stepped from the door, folowed by her father. Again they stopped and, after a minute of casual conversation, the marshal said, "If you could spare a minute, Judge, I'd like a word with you. It's important."

"Certainly," the Judge said. "Would you mind waiting in the lobby, Ann?"

"I most certainly would!" Her smile belied her words. "I'm sure Mr. Adams will see me home."

"I'd be glad to," Frank said, and looked toward the Judge.

The latter also conceded defeat. "Thank you," he said and succeeded in imbuing the words with a degree of warmth.

When they reached the front door, Ann turned. "You will come in this time?"

"I'd like to," he said. As he reached to open the door, she moved across in front of him and lifted her face toward his.

A moment later, Glynn opened the door and found them in each other's arms. "Holy cow," he said and closed the door quickly. They didn't hear-him.

THE ESTATE OF
THE BECKONING LADY
by Margery Allingham

The message in the faded flowers was clear: "Beware, a deadly foe lurks . . ." The warning was ignored—the English countryside seemed so peaceful and quiet. Expect for the still-warm corpse lying in a ditch nearby . . . .

95375—95¢

THE BIGAMOUS DUCHESS
by Muriel Elwood

A magnificent novel of the Royal Court. The whole of
London was at the feet of the fiery and beautiful
Elizabeth until a scandal threatened her downfall.

15144—$1.50